# THE FIRST-FORGED MIRROR

CIDNEY MAYES

CROW QUILL PUBLISHING

Book Cover by GetCovers

First Edition 2026

ISBN 979-8-9916361-5-5

Crow Quill Publishing

cidneymayes.com

# ALSO BY CIDNEY MAYES

## STARLIGHT AND SHADOWS

The Starlit Shadow

## THE NIGHTINGALE WITCHES

Season of Fire

*For those who have loved and lost.*

# PROLOGUE

Eiran Vael had read over forty accounts of the corruption over the course of his career, written by scholars who had observed it from the northern mouth of the Durnath Pass or from elevated vantage points with good tools and better sense. Every account without exception used the language of threat. *Devouring. Malevolent. A darkness that hungers.* He had always suspected this said more about the observers than the observed. Fear was a poor instrument. It introduced bias at the measurement stage, which contaminated everything downstream.

Standing in the third corruption zone with his notebook open and the mist pressing in at every edge of his vision, he found he had been right. The corruption was not malevolent. It was simply present, the way weather moved through a landscape, or in the way river in flood was present. It did not want anything from him, only spread into the available space and fill it.

He wrote this down. He had been writing things down for fourteen days and the notebook was nearly full. It was a problem he had anticipated. He reached into his satchel for a second notebook and noticed with the mild interest of a scholar cataloguing an unexpected variable that his hands were slower than usual.

*The corruption's effect on motor function,* he wrote, in the new notebook. *Onset: gradual. Fine motor skills affected before gross. Consistent with Meras's account of his own exposure, though Meras had been in the third zone significantly longer before extraction. I have been here forty minutes. Adjust timeline accordingly.*

He looked up from the writing.

The mist had thickened while he was working. He could see perhaps two meters in any direction, which was down from four meters when he had arrived at this position. The gradient reading on his instrument, Seraphine's instrument, showed the corruption density at this location was significantly higher than the mapped boundary had indicated. He noted this too. The mapping was wrong. The third zone extended further north than the initial survey team's data showed.

Someone had known this, or should have known this, and had sent them in anyway with the wrong numbers.

He filed that thought for later. Later required getting back to the camp, which required reversing his current bearing, which meant he needed to be able to see further than two meters.

He put the notebook away and picked up his compass.

His hands were considerably slower now. He noted this with mild interest, because the alternative was something less useful. Alarm spent energy, and energy was a finite resource. He required whatever energy remained for the return bearing.

The compass needle moved lazily. He wasn't certain if this was the instrument or his perception of it. He checked his gradient reader. The density in corrupted magic had increased again in the time it had taken him to reach for the compass, which meant either the mist was moving toward him or he had moved toward a denser pocket without noticing. The second option was more likely. The disorientation was affecting his sense of direction. So, he stopped moving.

Standing still was best. He knew this. When visibility was compromised and direction was uncertain, stillness was the right choice. The survey team knew his last recorded position. They would come to that position when he did not return by the agreed time. He needed only to remain at or near this position and wait.

He sat down on the ground, which was easier than standing and conserved energy, and took out his notebook again.

The instrument's pulse rate, he wrote, is registering at point-seven-two on the corruption density scale, which exceeds the threshold Seraphine specified for standard operation by a significant margin.

*I should have brought the calibration notes for high-density conditions. I told her I would not need them. I was wrong about that. I am making a note of it here so that when I report back, I can tell her I acknowledged the error in the field rather than only afterward, which I understand she will find marginally more acceptable than if I simply admitted it on return.*

He stopped writing. He had been thinking about the calibration notes, and then he had been thinking about Seraphine, and somewhere in the gap between those two thoughts he had lost the thread of why he was writing. He looked at the page. His handwriting was deteriorating. The last two lines ran downhill, and the letters were sloppy and slithered together. The s in Seraphine larger than it should have been, as though his hand had wanted to linger on it.

The mist pressed in.

He was aware that the corrupted air was affecting his cognitive function. He would have found this interesting if he were currently in a condition to find things interesting. The disorientation was not dramatic. There was no moment of sudden confusion, no clear before and after. It was more like the gradual loss of light at the end of a day. At some point it had become darker than it had been.

He tried to remember the return bearing. North-north-east. He was almost certain it was north-northeast. He checked the compass again. The needle was moving. Compass needles did not move when held still, they found their direction and held it. Either the corruption was inter-fering with the instrument's function, or he was not as still as he believed he was.

He put the compass away. He would wait for the survey team. They knew his position. They would come. He thought about Seraphine in the way he had gotten into the habit of thinking her name when he was working through something difficult. As though she were in the room, and he could turn to her with the problem, and she would set down her tool and diagnose it.

His hand shook. Fine motor function, he thought. Noted earlier. He had noted it earlier. It was in the notebook.

He opened the notebook to check and found he had diffi-culty reading his own handwriting in the lower half of the page. Not because of the light, which was the same diffuse grey it had been all day, but because the words were not resolving into meaning with their usual speed. He could see the letters. The letters were taking longer to become words.

North-northeast, he thought. He was almost certain.

The data he had collected. Fourteen days of gradient readings, the densest and most precise corruption boundary mapping anyone had attempted at close range. It was in the notebooks. Both notebooks were in his satchel. When the survey team came, they would take the satchel and the notebooks would be safe, and the data would be safe, and it would be enough to prove the boundary permeability theory completely.

The mist was very close now. He could see his hands and not much further. He could hear, at the edge of perception, the sound of the survey team's signal whistle.

Seraphine. He had not told her enough true things. He had told her many things, but not enough of the true ones. He had been waiting for the right moment, which was a habit he had always known was inefficient and had not fully corrected.

He was going to correct it when he returned.

The mist pressed in and the light that came through it was diffuse and directionless, the same from every angle. He couldn't hear the signal whistle, and he couldn't feel the cold the way he had been able to an hour ago. His hands had stopped shaking which was either good sign or a bad one.

North-by-northeast. I should have told her.

The mist was everything.

It was not frightening. He was noting this, in the part of him that was still noting things, because it seemed significant. The archive accounts of corruption exposure described fear as the predominant experience, and he was not afraid. He felt slow, and distant, and increasingly uncertain about north-northeast. It was more like the end of a long day than anything else. A heaviness of a body that has worked hard and is ready to stop, the way the quality of a late afternoon light changed from active to something softer.

He thought about Seraphine's light. The canal light, the way she talked about it, the reason she opened the windows every morning. *Glass lies,* she had said, or something like that. She had a specific word for it. He could not find the word now, but he knew the concept. She needed to see things as they were.

He had always liked that about her.

The mist was very still. The mist was everything, and then it was not anything. The notebook was still open on his knee, the pen still in his hand, and the last thing he had written was her name, larger than it should have been, as though his hand had wanted to linger on it.

It had been correct to linger.

He had been right about that, at least.

CHAPTER

# ONE

The first thing Seraphine did each morning was open the windows. Her workshop did not need the air. The ventilation system she'd built took care of that. She needed the light, pure and unfiltered. Light that shone through windowpane glass flattered and softened the edges of things and introduced a subtle dishonesty into the workshop that most people never noticed but quietly irked her.

She had tried over the years to explain this to various clients who had admired pieces in her workshop, then been surprised when the same object looked different in their own home. She told them it was the glass, always the glass, and they nodded in a way that suggested they were listening but not really hearing her. So, she stopped explaining and simply opened the windows each morning before she set to work, accepting that this was another small preference that made her better at her craft.

Grauradur's light in the early morning had the same shade as shallow water moving over pale stone. It that was neither warm nor cool, but it lent a sharp clarity to the things it touched.

Seraphine's workshop occupied the top two floors of a narrow pale stone building on the canal, which she owned outright and had spent the past twenty-two years modifying to suit her needs. The ground floor she rented to a bookbinder who kept considerate hours and never complained about the acrid smells that occasionally drifted down through the ceiling. He also left her a small jar of strawberry preserves on her doorstep every Winter Solstice without a note or explanation, which she appreciated more than she had ever said.

The upper floors were entirely hers. The main workroom ran the full length of the building and was lined with tools neatly arranged on the walls and shelves of ingredients that were perfectly logical to her, but no one else could seem to navigate successfully. The forge at the north had its own flue, which belched thick white smoke up and away from the building. Seraphine kept her living quarters on the middle floor, which consisted of a kitchen, a sitting room lined with well-read books, and a bedroom with a south-facing window. She had lived here for fifteen years, having purchased the building when she was twenty after successfully completing her apprenticeship, and knew every sound it made.

This morning she turned her attention to a set of resonance plates for a cartographer who needed to map a magical gradation across a large area. It was a commission, and Seraphine was nearly done with it. It was technically interesting and aesthetically undemanding, which suited her perfectly well.

She stood at the central bench, scarred with wear, and

held a fine-tipped calibration tool, making adjustments to the instrument that were so small they were only visible to someone who knew what they were looking for.

The plates were good and would do exactly what they were built to do for as long as they were cared for properly. It was all she ever promised, and more than what most clients expected.

Seraphine set the calibration tool down, a needle-nosed apparatus she had enchanted herself when the standard grade wasn't exact enough for her needs. She picked up the plates one by one, examining in the morning light. She turned them slowly, reading them in the way only she could. She saw past what they looked like and examined what they were. When she was satisfied, she wrapped them in cloth. She would set them in a wooden delivery crate labeled with the cartographer's name. Her work was interrupted when she heard the boy on the stairs.

She knew his tread. He visited his uncle in the bindery below most Tuesdays, a young fae child who had the energy of someone who found stillness physically painful. He was not supposed to come above the ground floor, but he came anyway, regularly, drawn by the general allure of a space he had been told was not for him.

Seraphine heard something she had not heard from him before. It was smaller and more defeated than his usual hovering. She set the plates down.

The boy was on the landing, holding a wooden horse with its foreleg snapped cleanly at the joint. He had not yet decided whether to cry. When he saw her, he straightened, preparing for the consequence of being caught.

Seraphine looked at the toy. A clean break at a stress

point, the grain splitting along a natural fault. It was going to break eventually.

"Give it here," she said, holding out her hand.

The boy extended it with shaking hands. Seraphine took it inside but did not close the door. She found a scrap piece with matching grain, cut a small reinforcing slat, applied a liquid adhesive, and held the joint for the time required. The boy stood in the doorway and watched without touching anything, his eyes wide.

She handed it back. "The leg is stronger now than it was. The break showed where the weakness was."

"Thank you," he said solemnly. He was still unsure if he would get in trouble for trespassing.

"Go back downstairs," she said. "Don't tell your uncle you were up here."

The boy nodded and ran all the way back down the stairs.

She returned to the resonance plates and thought nothing further about it. Seraphine washed her hands, adjusted the roll of her shirtsleeves, made tea, and stood at the open window while it steeped, watching the canal below.

Caeledrath, Grauradur's most illustrious city, was already in motion despite the early hour. Boats moved goods across the water, and fae crossed bridges that spanned the canal, carrying baskets of wares for market. The light off the water cast dappled, irregular shapes on the underside of the walkways, glinting in windows. Buildings of pale stone that scattered across the horizon as far as she could see glinted like polished jewels.

Seraphine watched with detachment, taking in the scene without judgement or opinion. This form of observation served her well in her work. It served her less well in her personal life. She never disagreed on that point when it was, occasionally, brought to her attention. It happened less now that she was established in her own workshop. Her mentor, Solvaine, who had taken her on as an apprentice when she was thirteen, had given her many quizzical looks over the years at her seeming inability to be what he called friendly and what she privately called excessively talkative.

Her tea was ready. As she picked up her cup, a handleless vessel from a potter's stall in the market she had purchased when she'd first opened her workshop, she heard footsteps on the stairs. Her building had an acoustic resonance that allowed her to identify most visitors by the sound of their approach. A moment later, a note slid under the door, bearing the Caeledrath University's seal.

The message was brief. A scholar in the Department of Ecology, Eiran Vael from the research quadrant, requested a consultation with her regarding a commission of an unusual nature. He had been referred to her specifically by a colleague in the artificer's guild, whose name Seraphine recognized and whose judgement she respected.

The commission, he wrote, was outside the scope of the available instruments, and he believed it required an artificer of significant skill. He had been advised that she was the best person for the job and would be grateful for an opportunity to discuss the parameters at her convenience.

She read it twice, which was once more than she typically read messages of this sort. Her eyes snagged again on the phrase *unusual nature.* It was a bold claim. Seraphine's entire body of work, all her skills, relied on crafting objects and tools that were, by definition, unusual. That, combined with *particular sensitivity* was either strictly a technical requirement or genuine flattery. It was true that she was significantly skilled for a fae of only thirty-five years. This was simple fact. She was able to craft things that Solvaine had only mastered after decades of study, which is why she'd been able to open her own artificer's workshop. The scholar's phrasing intrigued her more than she cared to admit. She wanted to see for herself which the scholar had meant. A magical ecologist who wanted an instrument outside of the standard scope...

Seraphine turned the question over in her mind with mild interest, then made up her mind. She went to her desk and wrote her reply, agreeing to a meeting at the end of the week. She sealed it and set it atop of the delivery crate for the morning post.

She refilled her tea, returned to her workbench, and began thinking about her next commission. A warding matrix for merchant family to keep them safe on their excursions to the northern territories, due in three weeks. There was the matter of a specific material that required resolving before she could begin. Seraphine pulled her notes toward her and picked up her pen.

The note from the university was already out of her mind before her tea had cooled.

# TWO

The scholar, Eiran Vael, arrived at the end of the week with his notebook already open.

Seraphine heard him on the stairs before she saw him. His tread was different than she was used to. Unhurried, but not tentative. He paused on the landing, as though he'd stopped to look at something, perhaps ensuring he had the right house. She set her tools down and waited, retying her pale blonde hair out of the way. When his knock finally came, it was in three short, confident, raps.

She called for him to enter and turned to the door.

He was younger than she'd expected for a scholar, and tall, with light brown hair that hung into hazel eyes, and a green coat that had seen better days. The left cuff was frayed at the edge in a way that suggested he either hadn't noticed or was completely unbothered by it. The right elbow was nearing a threadbare state. He had a leather satchel over one shoulder, and an open notebook in his left hand.

If he was a fae blessed with wings, she did not know. The confines of her workshop didn't allow for them to be present, so her clients were forced to will them away before they entered. Some of her more high-ranking clients were obviously disgruntled by this, but Seraphine found that they simply got in the way of everything. She had only let her wings emerge a handful of times in her life, mostly to check that she could still perform the function. They were pale and feathered, soft as down.

Sustained flight required a draw on magical reserves that most fae found impractical for anything beyond ceremony or emergency. The guild's transport regulations reflected this plainly. Wings were not a substitute for road travel, and any commission requiring the movement of materials or equipment beyond a quarter kilometer was to be conducted by conventional means. Seraphine had no use for her own wings them in her work, and so she did not waste magical energy summoning them when she went out. The canal boats were faster anyway.

The scholar was reading something from it as he came through the door, so the first thing he said was directed partially at the page.

"You're the one who made the Aldenmere lenses." He looked up. "The cartographic set. I've used them. They're extraordinary."

He stated his approval as if it were mere fact, and Seraphine could not tell if his words were mere observation or genuine flattery. "They do what they're made to do," she said simply.

"That's what makes them extraordinary." He crossed the workshop with his hand outstretched. "Eiran. Thank you for seeing me."

Seraphine shook his hand briefly, then directed him to one of the chairs she'd set next to her workbench.

He set his satchel on the floor and placed the open notebook on the bench between them, clearly used to conducting meetings around a shared page.

She looked at the notebook. Dense handwriting, diagrams tucked into the margins, and measurement table with figures crossed out and revised crowded the pages. He had done a good amount of preparation. She gave him credit for it.

"You mentioned that what you wanted to commission was outside the scope of available instruments."

He nodded. "Everything available can measure magical presence or absence. What I need it something that can measure gradation." He tapped one of the diagrams with a long finger. "The boundary region between Grauradur and Tenebris isn't a solid line. The corrupted and uncorrupted magic is a gradient, bleeding further into corruption by degrees. Those degrees behave differently from each other. All available apparatuses tell me where corruption is, but I need to know how much, and in what distribution, so I can map the patterns."

Seraphine studied the diagram, then pickup up the notebook without asking and read the measurement table. Her lips thinned.

"Your tolerance values are incorrect," she said.

"Which ones?"

"All of them." She flipped the notebook back towards Eiran. "You've made your calculations for a passive instrument. Something than only receives information. What you are describing requires both an input and output system. The output needs to read the return accurately at a given resolution. Your tolerances need to account for the instrument's own output interfering with what it's measuring in the environment."

A small line appeared between Eiran's brows. "That would significantly complicate the calibration."

"It would," Seraphine agreed.

"Could it be accounted for it in the design?"

"That's what I would build it to do."

He was silent for a moment. He looked at his figures and tapped his finger against the page.

Seraphine watched him run revisions in his head and trail his eyes across the notes he had made. She found, to her mild surprise, that she did not mind waiting.

"If it puts out a signal," he finally said, "and the corruption responds to that signal before the instrument can complete a reading—"

"It won't be a problem. I can calibrate its pulse rate. The corruption's response threshold is documented in your department's surveys. You cited it in your second footnote. Your measurements would be faster by about four points."

He studied her with an expression she could not read. "You read the surveys?"

"I read everything about a commission before I agree to take it."

"You agreed to this meeting before you knew what the commission would be."

"Which is why I read the surveys after. You did state that you were from the research quadrant." She pulled her own notes from a drawer, a single page with materials and some questions. "There are three things I need you to answer before I can confirm that the work is possible." She tossed her hastily braided hair over her shoulder.

They went through her questions. He provided detailed

answers when she needed them and was honest about the limits of his understanding. He said *I don't know* without any apparent discomfort, which was rarer than it should have been in her experience with clients. It was refreshing.

Eiran asked her two questions in return that were astute but revealed an assumption about the properties of resonance alloys that she corrected.

"That's not how resonance alloys behave under sustained output," she said.

"That's the standard position, but there is a paper from the Tenebris boundary surveys—"

"I've read it," Seraphine said. "The conditions in that paper were not controlled for ambient magical interference. The results do not apply outside of that one survey's context."

She paused at the hard look that flashed across her client's face. It was not anger, not at her. Perhaps disappointment. "The principle you're trying to apply is not wrong. The material is."

Eiran sat back in his chair and twisted his mouth to the side, as if deciding whether to argue or not and concluding that it wasn't worth it. "What material would you use for this instrument, then?"

Seraphine had listed possibilities on her note sheet. She spent the next twenty minutes discussing the merits of each one, which was not a conversation she expected to have with her client and did not really want it to end. He knew more about the theoretical behavior of magical materials than most fae she worked with. He did not possess artificer knowledge or practical experience, but he did have a genuine understanding of the underlying principles. She found she had to adjust her explanations far less than usual.

By the time they had revised the specifications for the commission, an hour and a half had passed. Seraphine only noticed when she glanced up and saw the angle of the light in the workshop had changed.

She set down her pen. "I can make this. I will need six weeks. I offer standard consultation terms, and I will need access to you for technical questions as they arise."

"Of course," Eiran agreed as his own pen moved across his notebook. Revising the tolerance figures, from what Seraphine could tell. "I'll need to be kept informed of design decisions that affect the output parameters. The instrument's behavior in the field will change what data I am able to gather."

Seraphine dipped her chin. "I will send notes as they become relevant."

He finally closed his notebook and reached for his satchel and coat, which he had removed when it became clear that the meeting was not going to be a brief one. "I'd rather come in, if it's all the same to you. Some of this is easier to discuss in front of the work."

Seraphine considered this request. It wasn't unreasonable. She had worked with involved clients before and found it as useful as often as she found it inconvenient. "Fine. The second and fifth days of the week would work."

Eiran stood and extended his hand again. "I'll see you next week."

She took his hand and shook it briefly. His grip was firm.

"Thank you," he said. "This was... well, *useful* isn't the right word."

"It's the right word."

He smiled, adjusted his satchel, and saw himself out.

Seraphine heard him on the stairs, the same unhurried

pace going down as coming up. She turned back to the bench.

The revised specifications sat in front of her. His handwriting alongside hers in the margins where they'd worked through the materials issue together. Seraphine looked at it for a moment, checking for anything they might have missed. The design was more interesting than she'd anticipated when she'd read the initial request. This was a genuine calibration challenge, and not something she could complete on instinct alone. It would require careful research and methodical building.

She picked up her pen and added a note she'd thought of while he was talking and hadn't interrupted to say.

The second chair sat at a slight angle where he'd pushed it back when he stood. Seraphine didn't notice, or didn't think about it, which amounted to the same thing.

She was already thinking about the resonance alloy.

# THREE

Eiran arrived on the predetermined day with questions about output frequency and left after forty minutes, satisfied. The next week he arrived with a different set of questions, stayed for an hour, and on his way out stopped to look at a piece on a display shelf near the door. A navigation compass Seraphine had made three years ago. The owner had requested a recalibration but never returned to collect it.

"What does it do?" Eiran asked.

She told him. He asked two more questions, neither of them relevant to his commission, and left when she didn't volunteer anything further.

The third day he came to check on the measuring instrument's progress, he reorganized her supply shelf.

Seraphine had stepped out to the floor below to retrieve a reference text. When she came back, Eiran stood at the east wall with a jar of copper filings in one hand. An expression of genuine puzzlement, and slight distress, plain on his face.

"Your system doesn't have a system."

"My system," she said, putting down the book and crossing her arms, "is not immediately apparent to someone who hasn't used it for fifteen years."

"The copper filings are before the iron powder and silver dust."

"Alphabetically."

He set the jar down, but not where he found it. "Alphabetically. And the resonance salts?"

"Are under R."

He stepped back and pointed. "On the bottom shelf."

"Because it comes after everything else, I use more frequently. Which are conveniently located on the top shelf."

Eiran looked at the shelf for a moment. Then, without asking her, he began to move things with methodical precision.

She should have stopped him. If anyone else had dared move her materials, she would have made them leave immediately. The system was hers and it had worked. The fact that it required explanation did not mean it was flawed. Seraphine opened her mouth to say so but became distracted by his hands.

They were quick and deliberate, setting each jar down with care before moving to the next. He read the labels before he moved anything, and he kept the jars level. These were not the hands of someone who was rearranging to impose his own logic on her space. He understood that the contents mattered, had watched how she'd used some of them, and was behaving accordingly.

Seraphine closed her mouth.

There was a specific kind of competence that Seraphine

recognized on sight, the way she recognized quality in materials. Not by what it looked like, but by how it moved. She did not have to agree with what he was doing to recognize that he was doing it well. So, she said nothing.

After he left, she moved the copper fillings back.

~

DURING HIS VISIT on the fourth week of the commission, Eiran commented on the windows. "You always work with them open?"

A brisk autumn wind blew into the workshop, made cooler by its passage over the canal. It had an edge to it, hinting of the colder days to come, but Seraphine did not mind. Cool air improved focus, and she required the light.

"I do," she said.

"It's cold."

"Yes."

Eiran looked at her, then walked to the bench and sat down. He opened his notebook and said nothing further about it.

Seraphine found his silence, or rather, his lack of argument more satisfying than she should have.

She turned her attention back to the magic gradation measuring device, which was nearing its most delicate stage, and quickly forgot about the exchange.

~

THE NEXT WEEK Eiran arrived before than their standing appointment was scheduled to begin. Seraphine wasn't ready for him, but he sat himself in a chair by the window and read without appearing to mind.

She finished was she was doing and turned to the instrument. They worked through the afternoon in silence that was comfortable without having to be negotiated. At some point, he made tea and set a cup beside her, without interrupting her work.

Seraphine drank it without acknowledging it. He'd made it with milk, and no sweetener. Just how she liked it. Neither of them remarked upon the gesture.

Soft autumn sunlight slid across the workshop, turning quickly into twilight. She had lost track of time, which often happened when her work was going well. When she surfaced from a tricky calibration sequence of the outer and innermost metal rings, it was dark outside and she was hungry, having not had anything but the tea since breakfast.

Eiran was still at the bench across from her, reading. His coat draped over the back of the chair, and he'd lit a lamp without her noticing.

"It's past seven," she announced.

He looked up, then at the window in mild surprise. He, too, had lost track of the hour. "So, it is."

Seraphine considered the situation. It was impractical to send him out at this hour when she was going downstairs to eat regardless. She was also not opposed to his continued presence. These were simply facts.

"I'm making dinner. It would be inefficient to make it for only one."

He accepted this, understanding the invitation was purely practical, rather than social. They ate in the kitchen on the floor below, a simple meal of bread and vegetable stew that she put together without ceremony. The conversation moved from the commission and its progress to Eiran's research, to a disagreement about the navigability of Tenebris's southern boundary that neither of them resolved before the dishes were done.

It was not until she was washing up that Seraphine noticed he'd reorganized her kitchen shelf at some point during the evening. He'd shuffled around the spices and dried herbs.

She turned to look at him, and he met her gaze with an expression of perfect innocence. She decided not to comment on his interference, for reasons she could not clearly articulate.

On the last meeting of their six-week schedule, the instrument was nearly finished. Eiran had been watching her for the better part of the afternoon, having arrived early once again.

He broke the silence from his chair by the window. "Can I ask you something? That isn't about the commission." The words left him quickly, which was unusual for him. He approached all things slowly, methodically. The rush told her he'd been thinking about saying this for a long time and had just decided to finally say it.

"You may ask," Seraphine said without looking up from the workbench.

"When you made the Aldenmere lenses. Were you working from your notes the whole time?"

She set her tool down. "I work from notes on every commission."

"That's not what I asked."

She looked up at that. He was watching her with the attention she had come to recognize as his most serious mode.

"No," she said, after a moment. "Not the whole time."

He nodded, as though this confirmed something, though he did not say what. He looked back at his notebook and made a notation, and the subject appeared to be closed.

Seraphine returned to the instrument.

She was aware, in the following hour, that he was still watching, though not intrusively. He read, made further notes, and was simply present. But she was aware of his attention in the specific way she was aware of good light, as a condition of the work rather than a distraction from it.

She picked up her needle-tipped tool and returned to the final calibrations, letting the enchantment move through her, down the tool which focused the spell, and into the device. The spells were stacked like sheets of vellum, one on top of the other. Disturbing one would send the entire thing cascading into a useless pile of carved metal and tiny screws. It required her utmost focus.

At some point she stopped consulting her notes. She did not decide to stop. Her hands simply knew the next step before she looked for it, and the step after that, and the work moved differently. The calibration sequence flowed from her rather than proceeded a step-by-step plan. She followed her instincts.

When she set the tool down the instrument was finished. Complete in the way that only certain pieces were complete, the kind that had gone somewhere she had not entirely planned.

Seraphine did not look at Eiran. She picked up what she

had made and examined it in the light. He remained silent, but she felt his inquisitive gaze on her.

As darkness descended fully, Seraphine told him to come back in four days to collect the completed instrument. She had not yet named it.

He gathered his coat and left with the easy pace that she had come to recognize.

As she closed the workshop for the evening, she thought about what he had asked. Seraphine couldn't come up with an answer that satisfied her. She was accustomed to knowing the answers to questions about her own work, and what she did not immediately know she was able to quickly find out through research.

That night as she lay in the dark, she went to bed that night thinking about the lenses, which she had not thought about in two years. About what that commission had asked of her that this one had not, until now.

She did not have a satisfying answer. She fell asleep still turning it over.

THE NEXT MORNING, Seraphine threw open the windows and went straight to her work bench. The instrument lay where she'd left it. The resonance alloy caught the early light, refracting it in the precise way she had calculated for. She turned it slowly, looking past the surface of it and peering into what it *was*.

It was good work. Careful, precise, and exactly within the parameters she had set for it. Only a few more adjustments were required.

She made a briefly noted her progress on her schematics

and picked up her tools. Seraphine began to work differently than she had been these past few weeks. She slowly, gradually, brought down the barriers of questioning, logic, and tables to let than indeterminate part of her float to the surface. By midmorning, she was no longer consulting her notes.

Seraphine finished the commission two days later. It sat on her workbench, waiting for Eiran to come collect it. A disc of resonance alloy in a dark steel frame, the alloy itself the color of deep water, neither silver nor grey but something between the two that shifted slightly depending on the angle of the light. The base ring was calibrated in increments too fine to read without knowing what to look for. At the instrument's center, a point of inlaid silver shimmered, the way a fixed star looks brighter against a moving cloud. When it was active, the silver point pulsed at a rate just below what the eye could comfortably track, and the alloy around it seemed to breathe.

She used to the spare hours to check it, and check it again, which was not something she typically did. When a piece was finished, it was done. She tested her work during its making, verifying that all was in order during each stage of creation. But she checked this instrument anyway, noting the calibration and output frequency, which held to the tolerance she had first specified. It ended up being considerably finer than Eiran's original parameters, or what he had asked for. She had built it to do what the work required, rather than what the brief demanded, like always.

Eiran arrived, climbing up the stairs with his slow, unhurried pace. She let him in and walked to the bench where the instrument lay gleaming.

She talked him through its operation. The activation sequence and calibration procedure, maintenance requirements, how to tell if the output frequency drifted, and how to fix it.

He listened with rapt attention and waited until she had finished speaking to ask his questions. "If the pulse rate can be adjusted, can it be slowed as well as increased?"

Seraphine lifted the instrument and placed it in his hands. She then showed him where to make the necessary adjustments. "The secondary ring on the base can be shifted counterclockwise."

"And if I slow it below the corruption's response threshold deliberately—"

"You'd be giving the corruption time to react to the pulse before the reading completes. The data would be compromised."

"Or it would give me something different than what I am currently trying to measure," he countered. He turned the apparatus, squinting at it as it caught the light. "A corrupted area's reaction pattern to a magic stimulus might be as informative."

Seraphine had not considered this application for the tool she had made. It was not what she had built it for, but the instrument would do as Eiran suggested. He was right that the data would be different, rather than wrong. It was only a question of how the device was used. She turned over the puzzle briefly in her mind, before alighting on the necessary steps.

"That would require a separate calibration protocol. I can write one for you."

He cradled the device between his hands as if it were a bird's egg instead of something made of alloy and metal. "Thank you. I'd appreciate it."

Seraphine wrote out the protocol while he waited. The task took ten minutes, as she had to reference one of her more obscure tables before setting ink to paper. When she was finished, she handed the scroll to him.

Eiran took it and ran his thumb over the resonance alloy, as if feeling for something rather than simply examining the surface.

"This is exactly what I needed," he said, looking up at her. "The active pulse design changes what I'll be able to conclude from the data significantly." He paused, as if carefully weighing his words. "This is better than what I originally asked for."

Seraphine rubbed a splotch of ink from her finger, not quite sure how it had gotten there. "It's what the commission required."

Eiran looked at her through lashes that were full and dark. "Yes, that's what I mean."

A silence hovered between them. The pause that occurred when deciding on which path to take, whether to stay or to go. The commission was complete. Their relationship was at its natural closure. But Seraphine sensed that Eiran did not want it to close entirely.

"Did you name it? The instrument?" he finally asked.

"No, I hadn't." A name hadn't come to her while the measuring device sat on her bench. But seeing it in Eiran's hands, who she had come to understand as methodical, curious, and a little stubborn over these past few weeks, the instrument came more fully to life. He would use it research, and it would do what she designed it to do. "But I think Thaumic Meridian seems fitting.

He looked at the device in his palm. "It does."

He settled the invoice, packed the Meridian into the cushioned carrying case she'd made for it, shook her hand, then left.

Seraphine heard him pause on the landing, as he always did, but he lingered for a half-moment longer than usual. The stairs creaked as he descended, and the echo of the closing front door reverberated through her ribcage.

The workshop was empty, save for her. Just as it always had been.

Seraphine turned back to her bench and began clearing it, readying it for the next commission.

THE WARDING MATRIX took three weeks and was straightforward enough that her hands knew what to do on their own, leaving her mind free to go elsewhere. What she kept thinking about was exactness and what it served. She did not give herself explicit permission to ruminate on the question, yet her thoughts kept flitting back to it like a magnet drawn to its pair.

She finished the matrix, delivered it, and took on two smaller commissions. Variations of navigation compasses for merchants who were traveling northward. She was midway through the first when she heard a tread on the stairs she recognized.

Seraphine had the door open before he had the chance to knock.

Eiran stood on the landing with his satchel, notebook, and too-worn coat. "Recalibration question," he said.

Seraphine moved aside to let him in.

The recalibration questions took eleven minutes to explain. The three hours that followed covered the behavior of the Thaumic Meridian in Eiran's first field test, a discrepancy in his boundary mapping data that turned into a problem neither of them could fully resolve, and a debate on whether this discrepancy indicated an error with the Meridian or an anomaly in the corruption pattern.

Eiran found the idea of the anomaly more likely, and more interesting, than the idea of some flaw with the device. Seraphine found this idea interesting despite herself.

As golden autumn light moved across the workshop, the conversation about his research changed gradually, moving to the broader territory of what he was studying and why.

He talked about Tenebris the way a naturalist might speak of difficult terrain. He did not paint a romantic picture of it, but he spoke with the enthusiasm of someone who found it utterly fascinating. The corruption wasn't a problem to him so much as it was a phenomenon.

She understood the distinction. Seraphine had her own version of it in the objects she was drawn to making verses the ones she made for commission. The thing that pulled her mind without demanding practical reason.

Eiran spoke of corruption as merely another natural phenomenon, like thunderstorms or a blizzard. When other fae spoke of the corruption, their voices were tinged with fear. It was a threat to them, to the magic that they needed to survive. Stories of corruption, a hungry and vengeful force that was determined to swallow and destroy pure magic, were often used a story to scare young fae, or caution folk against traveling south.

Seraphine, who had never observed corruption herself, did not have a strong opinion of it. It was something that existed beyond the mountainous border that separated Grauradur and Tenebris. High peaks and craggy terrain kept the corrosive force at bay. Only scholars, naturalists, traders, merchants, and magic experimenters had any desire or reason to go close to the corruption zones.

When it became too dim and Seraphine reached for the oil lantern, Eiran stood.

"I should go," he said. He dragged his satchel over his shoulder and tucked his notebook under his arm. He bid her goodnight and left.

Seraphine closed the door and stood in the middle of the workshop. She wrapped her arms around herself and studied the space. Everything was in its place. Her materials, the bench, and the furnace which kept the room from being too cold with the windows open. But the room felt larger than usual.

She closed the windows and went downstairs to make dinner, setting aside the observation to think about at another time. She did not want to think about it, or what it meant, now.

CHAPTER

# FIVE

The chair by the window became Eiran's.

She didn't decide this outright. It happened the way most things happened with Eiran. It was gradual, then suddenly an established fact she hadn't been consulted about. He simply always sat there when he came, and Seraphine simply left it clear for him. At some point she stopped thinking of it as the chair by the window and started thinking of it as Eiran's chair.

He always came on the same day, early in the week. A habit developed over the six weeks of his commission. Then he occasionally stopped by on other days for reasons that became less technical as the weeks passed and the first kiss of winter frost clung to the windowpanes. Eiran came with a text he thought she'd find interesting, or a study on a material he knew she often used. One afternoon he came by simply because he'd been passing by, on his way to the river market for groceries. He always had a reason for his visits.

The reasons, over time, became less the point.

A book appeared on the windowsill. Eiran left it there,

34

face down, when she'd called him to come and give his assessment on the weight of a current commission — was it too heavy? The book stayed there after he left for the night and Seraphine didn't mention it or move it.

After that, there was always a book on the sill. Not always the same one. She read the titles without really meaning to, and began, also without planning to have opinions on his reading.

One afternoon, Eiran set his notebook beside the plain ceramic pitcher she used for holding milk, bringing it up from the kitchen whenever she made tea. She set the pitcher on the work bench; he placed his notebook next to it. Somehow, after that, his notebook always went next to the pitcher. Seraphine moved the vessel one day, just to see what would happen. Eiran set his notebook down, registered the absence of the pitcher with a brief pause, and relocated both notebook and pitcher to the far end of the work bench as if this were the most reasonable solution.

These were small things that Seraphine cataloged. She noted them precisely, and without immediate interpretation, as she did with all things.

On an evening in early winter, Eiran invited her to a gathering at the university.

"There's a colloquium at the end of the week," he said, not looking up from his notebook. "Faculty and associates. You should come."

Seraphine stoppered the jar of silver powder. "I'm not faculty or an associate."

"You're my instrument maker. That's close enough." He

turned the page. "It starts at seven. I'll meet you at the east entrance."

She looked at the back of his notebook, jar of powder still in hand. "You're assuming I want to attend a university colloquium."

"I am assuming you'll find it more interesting than you expect." He looked up then, briefly. His hazel eyes were bright. "You can leave whenever you'd like. No one will be offended."

Seraphine did not immediately agree, but on the evening of the colloquium, she traded in her usual work pants and shirt for a woolen dress and put on her coat and gloves. As she stepped out into the frosty night, she told herself this was a professional decision. She was aware that on some level, it was not entirely that.

Eiran was already at the east entrance when she arrived, talking to a colleague. He had exchanged his green coat for a dark jacket that fit him considerably better. One she suspected he had borrowed. Both had manifested their wings. Eiran's were dark brown, shifting to black, the same shade as his hair. His colleagues were the color of wet stone, dark and severe. She should have known that most fae here would chose to display them. She forgot, sometimes, how rare it was that everyone who entered her workshop did not bear their wings. It was a condition she forced on others, for safety as well as convenience, that was not typical in Grauradur.

Seraphine touched the end of her hasty braid with gloved fingers. She had not considered that she might need to dress nicely for this event.

Eiran saw her and crossed the entrance hall with easy purposefulness. He had expected her to come and was unsurprised, and pleased, that she had. She felt, in equal measure, annoyed by his presumption and something warmer that she could not name.

Eiran introduced her to several colleagues, who received her with the interest of academics encountering someone from outside their institution. They were curious, slightly formal, and warmed when the conversation found its footing, or when they realized she was the alchemist who had crafted some of the instruments they used in their work. She talked to a cartographer who had used the Aldenmere lenses in the field who had specific and useful things to say about them. A boundary surveyor whose work intersected with Eiran's, and who held strong opinions about the inadequacy of current corruption-mapping capabilities, spoke to them for several minutes. She found herself agreeing with him on a few points, purely on technical grounds.

She ate something from a passing tray, and accepted a short glass of amber liquor, which she tasted but did not finish.

Eiran moved through the room with the ease of someone who clearly belonged. He stopped frequently, asked questions of everyone he talked to with the same intense attention Seraphine had come to know in her workshop, so that each one briefly believed they were the most interesting person in the room.

Seraphine couldn't help but compare him to the Meridian he had commission from her. He put something out, read what came back, and was genuinely interested in what the return signal said. She was not like that. She knew this without finding herself wanting. It was simply the way she was. She interacted purposefully, with specific intention, converting energy for when it mattered and spending it fully when it did.

These were not the same approach and produced different results. Seraphine understood, as she watched him talk to a junior researcher with the same quality of attention he gave to anyone, that she found his approach genuinely interesting in a way that had nothing to do with professional admiration.

Then at eight o'clock, Eiran took his place at the podium. He had failed to mention, perhaps purposefully, that the colloquium would be centered around his work tonight. He gave a brief presentation about his boundary mapping data. He had three years of it, she realized as she listened, compiled from remote surveys, secondhand accounts, and readings from the Thaumic Meridian she had built for him. He laid it all out with patient precision, having built his case for long enough to know exactly which evidence belonged where.

Eiran argued for a more formal expedition to map the boundary of corrupted and pure magic between Grauradur and Tenebris. Close observation of the southern corruption areas. He wanted the research to get as close as possible, not to gather readings taken from a careful distance. He wanted data sufficient to make inaction about the corruption and its growing closeness politically difficult. He mentioned the last part without raising his voice, which made it land harder than if he had.

Seraphine stood at the back of the room and watch his colleagues. Some leaned forward. An elderly man with silver spectacles sat at the front with his arms crossed and a grimace carved into his face. Two junior researchers took notes with frenetic energy. Most of the room was somewhere in between. Attentive, uncertain, but not yet committed to agree with him or dismiss his case entirely.

Eiran did not appear to see any of this. He presented his findings and his case without performance, as though the information itself was interesting enough without embellishment.

She found herself turning his argument over, testing its joints and finding them sound. Seraphine had known pieces of this, the boundary permeability theory, the corruption mapping limitations, and the inadequacy of remote surveying, from their conversation these past months. Assembled in sequence, it became a complete and serious thing and deserved a room better than this one.

When he finished, there were questions. Some were genuine, others skeptical. Eiran answered them with even patience, not conceding where he shouldn't and recognizing uncertainty where it existed. The faculty member with the scowl and folded arms said something that not quite a comment and not quite dismissal. Eiran looked at him with perfect, courteous attention and responded with unflappable politeness.

At the back of the room, Seraphine looked down at her glass, still nearly full, to avoid anyone see her small smile.

A FEW DAYS LATER, Seraphine was working on another commission, a locating charm. Her mind was elsewhere, running without direction, until it snagged on a problem Eiran had described during his lecture at the university. There was a limitation with the Meridian she'd made for him in dense corruption areas, where the ambient magical interference compressed the pulse return in ways that made the gradient data harder to read. He hadn't asked her to solve this problem. It wasn't her commission to solve.

She solved it anyway.

Not the full problem, as that would require modifications to the Meridian itself, which would be a separate conversation. But she could make a small, supplementary piece. A filter to attach to the instrument in dense zones to dampen the ambient interference without affecting the pulse output. It would need to be made of resonance alloy. A thin, specific grade that wouldn't itself interfere with the Meridian. She knew the grade she had in stock. Her hands were already moving toward it before she decided to begin.

The task took most of the afternoon. When she finished, she held it up to the clear winter light. A small oval of ally set in a plain wire mount, no larger than a coat button. There was nothing ornamental about it, but it worked. She could feel that it worked.

Seraphine set it on the corner of her bench.

She almost didn't give it to Eiran when he stopped by the next day. It was not a commission. She had not been asked to make it. The line between useful professional courtesy and something else, was less defined than she would have liked.

Eiran arrived, sat in his chair, and opened his notebook. Seraphine picked up the filter and extended it to him without explanation.

He took it gently between his fingers and turned it over carefully in the same way he had handled the Meridian when it had been completed, feeling for what it was rather than looking at the surface of it.

"For the interference problem. In dense zones," she said without preamble.

Eiran was quiet for a moment. Then he looked up at her.

A small line appeared between his brows. "You made this on your own time."

"I finished with a commission ahead of schedule."

"Seraphine."

The way he said her name cause a ripple of warmth to float through her suddenly, like a bubble of heated metal popping when it met cool air.

He closed his hand around the filter. "Thank you."

She picked up her tools. "The wire mount will need replacing eventually. Bring it back when it starts to tarnish."

"I will," he said. He set it on top of his book on the windowsill where it remained for the rest of the afternoon.

AFTER A WINTER that was warmer than previous winters had been, with little snow and bright sunshine that shone of the canal in diamond-bright streaks, Seraphine had grown quite used to Eiran's company. It was six months to the day she had received his letter requesting a commission, that he told her about the expedition.

Seraphine was working at her bench, finishing a piece. They shared a companionable silence that did not require anything from either of them.

"The council approached me," he said, not looking up from his book. "About a formal research expedition."

She kept her eyes on her work, gripping a thin piece of filament with her tweezers. "Into Tenebris." It was not a question.

"Southern boundary regions," he confirmed. "Three months. Perhaps four. It will be a proper survey. A close observation of corruption patterns rather than remote mapping." He turned a page. "They want data they can use for policy decisions. They asked me to lead it."

Seraphine did not say anything.

He looked up then. She kept her eyes fixed on the task in front of her.

"I haven't agreed yet," he said.

Seraphine put down the tweezers. "That's your decision to make."

Eiran closed his book and swung his leg off the arm of the chair, planting both feet firmly on the floor. "I thought you'd have an opinion."

Seraphine swallowed. "I have opinions about resonance calibration and material grades. And whether windows should be open in October." She reached for a jar of tiny screws and a screwdriver that was as thin as a needle. "Tenebris expeditions are outside of my area."

He continued to watch her for a moment. She felt him watching her as she twisted the screw. She did not stop her work, keeping her attention fully on it, equal to the attention he was now giving her spine.

"I'll let you know what I decide."

A beat passed, heavy and more strained than any silence had been between them. Seraphine cleared her throat. "Do you think this is too small? The captain said he wanted a smaller model, but I don't want it to get lost."

The floorboards creaked as Eiran moved to stand over her shoulder. She held up the sextant. It was smaller than she typically crafted them, but its size did not diminish its function. She knew it was not too small.

"If he's a careful man, I don't think it will be a problem."

She tore her eyes from the metal instrument in her hands, lifting her gaze to meet his.

There were shadows in his eyes. A lump formed in Seraphine's throat. She nodded, blinked, and picked up her screwdriver, checking the tightness of the screw she had just placed perfectly.

Eiran moved back to his chair and threw one leg over its arm.

Seraphine did not know why she had changed the subject, nor explain the lump in her throat, hard as iron.

She focused on oiling the hinges of the sextant until the tightness left her.

CHAPTER

# SIX

S pring arrived in Grauradur slowly, then all at once. The sunlight turned warm, heating the workshop during late afternoons, and a softer breeze blew in from off the canal.

Eiran had been there since mid-morning. The work they were doing, a recalibration of the Thaumic Meridian's filter which had begun to tarnish as Seraphine had said it would, finished around noon. The afternoon morphed into what had now become a comfortable routine for them. Eiran read in his chair, and Seraphine turned her attention to a small warding object for a client she liked. The workshop was peaceful and still.

Seraphine made tea and set Eiran's cup on the windowsill without interrupting him. She paused, accepting the ease of the small exchange. Eiran continued to read, not registering that she lingered nearby. Her cheeks flushed inexplicably as he traced a long finger down the page, and she quickly turned back to her work.

Spring light came through the windows at a new angle, brighter than the pale light of winter. It caught the bench in a way that made the grain of the old wood look like veins.

"Can I ask you something?"

"You may," she said, pulling a spool of wire toward her.

Eiran closed his book with his finger marking the page.

"Do you ever get lonely here?"

Seraphine kept her hands moving as she worked through the question. He had asked her plainly, and she would give him an honest answer in return.

"No," she said. "Not in a way I've ever found troubling."

"There is a distinction there."

Seraphine clipped the wire and returned the spool to its place on the second shelf. "There's always a distinction." She looked at the piece on the workbench. "I've lived alone for a while. I know what it feels like, and what I've traded for it, and on most days, it is reasonable to me."

"Only most days?"

"Yes."

Eiran thought for a moment. He remained in his chair, finger marking his place, and watched her hands still above her work. "I ask because I've been trying to work out something for a while now. I've concluded that the direct approach is probably more efficient than an indirect one, given what I know about you."

Seraphine looked up from her bench and was taken aback by the seriousness in Eiran's face. His brow was slightly furrowed in the way it did when he was trying to understand a problem.

"I find myself arranging my week, my whole life, around when I may visit you here."

Seraphine's stomach pitched.

"That has been true for some time," Eiran continued, his nerves betrayed by the shift in his tone. There was a current of urgency in how he spoke, as swift as the spring rains that rushed in the canal. "And I think you probably know that. I think I've been waiting to see if you'd say something about it, and I've concluded that you won't. To be fair, it's consistent with everything I know about you. So, I'm saying something about it instead."

His hands gripped his book cover. "I'm not sure what I'm asking exactly. I know what I'd like the situation to be, but I'm less certain what it is."

Seraphine studied him. The way his soft hair fell into his eyes, his worn green coat tossed casually over the back of his chair, the way he kept his finger on the page of his book, as though he intended to go back to it when this was done. As though what he had said could be slotted into an afternoon without disrupting everything that came after.

She thought about the chair he sat in, how it had become his. The milk jug and the journal, and the resonance filter she had made him even though he had not asked her for it. About the colloquium, and how he had made her lower her chin and smile into her glass.

She flexed her fingers. "I—" she stopped cleared her throat. "I don't know what to do with people." The admission came out more plainly that she had intended, but it was the truth. "I know how to work and be precise about things that I am making. People are less defined. Their tolerances are harder to read."

Eiran gave her a half smile. "I've noticed that about you. I find it..." he paused, searching for the same accuracy and honesty that she had given him. "I find it one of the more interesting things about you. Your precision. It's not coldness, even when it might look like it from the outside."

A warm current moved through Seraphine, the same that surged when she was in the thick of her work, her notes and tables set aside because her mind, her hands, knew what to do. "You have been trying to read my tolerances."

"For about the past eight months, yes."

"And?"

"I think they are finer than you let on. The work you do when you trust them is extraordinary." He held her gaze steadily. "I'm not only talking about the artificer work."

Seraphine rose from the bench and crossed to where he was sitting. She looked out the open window where fae moved over bridges, barges moved under them, through the canal. Petals from spring blossoms, delicate white and soft pink, blew from one of the trees.

"I didn't say anything because I wasn't sure what I would be saying. I like to be sure before I speak."

Eiran stood and joined her at the window, following her gaze with his own. "Are you sure now?" he asked softly.

From the corner of her eyes, Seraphine noted the way the light struck his face, brightening his irises and making the subtle gold in his hair shine. "I am sure enough."

He smiled and shifted his weight. Their shoulders brushed together, then the outsides of their little fingers.

Seraphine was startled by how warm he was.

When she did not move away, he wrapped his finger around her own, threading them together. They remained at the window for some time, watching the bustle of the streets and canal below, enjoying the closeness they now shared.

When he left, it was quite late. The streets had gone quiet. Seraphine stood at the open window and listened to his footsteps on the cobblestones below until she couldn't hear them anymore.

She smiled and shut the window before she went to bed.

# CHAPTER
# SEVEN

Seraphine stopped thinking of tea as something she made for herself and happened to make Eiran a cup because he was there.

He started coming to the workshop in the morning. She put the kettle on and set out two cups. At some point, she started doing it when she heard him on the stairs, then she did it on days he wasn't coming, simply because her hands had grown accustomed to preparing two cups of tea instead of one. She did not stop putting out two cups but simply noted it and filed it away with the other changes in her habitual behavior.

THE DISCUSSION about the window shifted a few weeks later. Eiran would arrive to the workshop, and the windows would be open. He would look at them, then at Seraphine. She would look back at him, unmoving, and the entire issue of the windows would happen in that exchange without either of them saying a word about it, which was its own sort of efficiency.

Occasionally, they used more than glances to address the window problem.

"It's raining," Eiran said one morning, standing in the doorway with his coat damp at the shoulders and his hair clinging to his brow.

"It's sprinkling," she said without turning away from the bench.

"Your bench is going to get wet."

"It's been wet before." It was only the far end of it, closest to the window. Her materials were safely stored in glass vessels, her work placed in the center of the bench, away from errant mist or raindrops.

Eiran set his satchel down, then looked at the windows. He whipped his head to Seraphine, who continued to work, then back at the windows. He walked to the chair, then opened his notebook.

Five minutes later, Seraphine heard him get up. She assumed he was going to close the windows, and she prepared her response. Instead, he left the workshop. She heard his steps descend to the floor below, heard the close of a cabinet in the kitchen. He came back with a cloth, draped it over the end of the bench nearest the window. Then he sat in his chair.

A comfortable silence bloomed in the workshop.

"Thank you," she said.

"You're welcome."

The windows stayed open, and her bench stayed dry. They did not discuss the matter further, which meant that they would discuss it again in a slightly different form, indefinitely, because that was the nature of their opinions and arguments that weren't really about the thing, they were about.

Seraphine found she didn't mind.

THE GREEN COAT she had opinions about from the beginning. It was not that it was worn. Worn things had integrity and had earned their state through use. It was that it had reached a condition of wear that had become structural, the kind where the coat was being held together by familiarity rather than fiber and thread. The right elbow had been a concern since the day she met him. Now a button replaced with one that didn't quite match, a small repair at the collar that had been made by someone who was not a tailor joined the growing list of failings.

"You could replace it," Seraphine said one morning, watching him drape it over his chair.

Eiran shrugged. "I like this one."

"I can see that. It's falling apart."

"I prefer to think of it as acquiring character." He sat down and opened his notebook. "You have opinions about a coat."

Seraphine's mouth twisted into a wry smile. "I have opinions about most things."

"I know." He looked up. "Would it help if I told you my mother made it?"

Seraphine studied the coat and took in this new piece of information. It did not change the fact that the coat was still barely serviceable. "It does not change the status of your coat," she said. "But I suppose I understand why you still wear it."

He smiled at his notebook, and she turned back to the bench.

She did not mention the coat again, and found a fondness nestled in her chest whenever she looked at it, or him wearing it.

⁓

ONE AFTERNOON, Eiran brought papers from his department rather than his notebook. A stack of survey reports he needed to cross-reference. He started quietly, half under his breath, and Seraphine assumed he wasn't aware of it. She said nothing, and by the time she realized he was fully aware and simply unbothered, she had become interested in what he was reading.

He had a good voice for it. Unhurried, with the natural emphasis of someone who understood what they were reading rather than performing it. Seraphine found she could work and listen simultaneously. The two activities occupied different enough parts of her attention that neither of them suffered.

Eiran seemed to arrive at the same conclusion, but asked her just the same, having found that directness with her was the most efficient. "Does it bother you?"

"No," she replied, shaking grams of copper filings onto her scale. "You read well. And I am interested in the subject."

He nodded once and continued reading. He read aloud often after that, the rhythm of his voice adding to the texture of the day.

Seraphine learned more about the corruption boundary behavior in those afternoons than she had from any deliberate study. She did not tell him this, but she suspected he knew.

Spring bloomed fully, and time moved peacefully to early summer. The days were warm, the nights cool, benefitting from the soft winds that blew off the canal. Lavender, rose, and peach stained the sky at twilight.

One morning when the air was thick with humidity, Seraphine and Eiran stood on opposite sides of the workbench. Eiran had been recalibrating the Thaumic Meridian and had used a cloth she would not have used, one take from the rack by the forge.

"Not that cloth," Seraphine said.

He looked down at the fabric square. "What's wrong with it?"

"It's too coarse for that grade of alloy. You'll introduce micro-abrasions in the surface and compromise the output consistency over time."

"The weave on this is finer than the standard workshop cloth," Eiran countered.

"It's finer than the standard workshop cloth and still too coarse for resonance alloy at that grade. They're not the same comparison." Seraphine crossed to the rack and took down another cloth, a softer one with a closer weave that she kept separately for exactly this purpose and held it out to him. "This one."

Eiran took it, looked at it, then looked at the one he'd been using. "The difference in weave density is marginal."

"It's sufficient. Resonance alloy at that grade is worked to tolerances that most cloths will degrade over repeated cleaning. It's not immediately visible. It accumulates," she countered.

"What's your evidence for that?"

She looked at him and crossed her arms. "Twenty-two years of working with resonance alloy."

"That's an appeal to authority," Eiran said. Mirth danced in his eyes.

"It's an appeal to authority *and* direct empirical experience, which is a stronger position than theoretical disagreement from someone who has been handling resonance alloy for approximately eight months," Seraphine countered.

"The length of time I've been handling it isn't relevant if my reasoning is sound."

"Have you read Carrath's work on fine alloy degradation?"

"I've read Carrath. His test conditions used a standard cleaning cycle once every three weeks. How often are you cleaning this?"

She paused. "Once a week."

"Then Carrath's degradation curve doesn't apply at your cleaning frequency. The abrasion risk he documents is cumulative above a threshold you're not reaching."

"Carrath's threshold is based on a different grade of alloy than this one."

"He doesn't specify the grade."

Seraphine clicked her tongue. "He doesn't specify it because he was working with the standard commercial grade, which is what his institution used. This is a finer grade. The threshold is lower."

Eiran peered at the filter, then at her. "You're extrapolating from an unspecified variable," he said.

"I'm applying twenty years of material knowledge to a gap in Carrath's methodology."

"Which brings us back to the appeal to authority," he said triumphantly.

"Which I have already told you is also an appeal to empirical experience, which is not the same thing as authority or extrapolation, and all three support the same conclusion." She uncrossed her arms. "Use the right cloth."

He turned the marginally softer cloth over in his hands. His brow furrowed as he reassessed his position without wanting to reassess it too quickly.

"What if I grant the grade variable," he said, "but contest the cleaning frequency threshold? If Carrath's curve doesn't apply, there's no established degradation rate for this grade at weekly cleaning. You might be overstating the risk significantly."

"I might be."

His head snapped up. His eyebrows were raised.

"I could be overstating it," she said, unfazed by his shock at her concession, "and I am still correct that the coarser cloth introduces unnecessary risk when the right cloth is sitting on the rack three feet away. So, the practical conclusion is identical regardless of whether the degradation risk is large or marginal."

Seraphine realized she was enjoying herself. Not despite the disagreement, but because of it. He was wrong and she was telling him so, and he was listening, weighing her points with the same attention he gave to everything. He opposed her without dismissing her, holding his position without requiring her to abandon hers.

She had disagreed with people for decades, but it had never felt like this. Like it was a place two people were occupying together rather than a territory one of them had to win.

"That's actually a good argument," he said, and put down the cloth he'd originally selected.

"I know."

"I still think you're overstating the abrasion risk."

"I know you do." Seraphine smiled and returned to the workbench. She picked up her tool.

"Noted," he said.

She looked at him over her shoulder, and he was looking back at her with the expression she'd stopped pretending she didn't look for. Seraphine faced forward and returned to her work with a slight smile.

# EIGHT

The symposium was held in the university's largest lecture hall, which was full in a way that suggested Eiran's reputation preceded him more than Seraphine had realized. The colloquium was one thing; this was another entirely.

She took a position at the back of the hall where she could see the entire room. The rows of faculty, researchers, and attendees sorted themselves by academic allegiance without saying a word. Some leaned forward with eager anticipation. Others crossed their arms, having already made up their minds before the seminar even began. The larger middle ground of people, who had come to be convinced either way, kept their faces arranged in neutrality. They understood that the wrong opinion, when held publicly, had professional consequences. For Seraphine's perch, it appeared that senior members of the university displayed their wings, while junior researchers, students, and lesser-ranked staff kept theirs away. This was practical, as there was a finite amount of space, even in the lecture hall, but spoke to the hierarchies within the university.

Eiran stood at the podium and arranged his notes with ease. He didn't really need the notes. He comfortable enough with the material that they were more of a formality. He wore his good jacket again, the one she suspected he'd borrowed from someone else, and his wings were on display.

The room hushed as the clock struck six. Eiran began without preamble. The data came first. Three years of boundary mapping, the Meridian readings, and the gradient distributions across some sections of southern corruption zones. He noted the change in granular data in the past year, citing the creation of Seraphine's Thaumic Meridian as pivotal in the success of its gathering. He presented all his without dramatics, in the same manner he read aloud in the workshop. The numbers were good. The kind that made a case before anyone had drawn a conclusion from them, the kind that required active resistance to dismiss.

The corruption was, indeed, spreading.

A white-haired senior faculty member in the third row raised his hand before Eiran had moved to his conclusions. "Your gradient mapping assumes a consistent corruption rate across the boundary region," he said. "The Halveth surveys from documented significant variance. How do you account for that?"

Eiran answered the question smoothly. If he was irritated at being interrupted, he did not show it. "The Halveth surveys used passive instruments with a response threshold too broad to detect gradient variation below a certain scale. What was recorded in those surveys forty years ago as variance was actually measurement limitation, not actual inconsistency in the corruption pattern. The instrument I'm using, the Thaumic Meridian, operates at a resolution four times finer, and the gradient is consistent. Earlier data couldn't see it."

The faculty members expression did not change in any way that constituted as concession. "That is a significant claim about survey data this institution has used reliably for decades. *Established* survey data."

"It's a testable one. The methodology is in the appendix."

The man glanced at the copy of papers he had been given upon entry. He did not open it and sat back in his chair.

More questions followed from the group of people who sat with their arms folded, their brows furrowed. They were not inquiries, but performances of skepticism. They rose objections to signal their doubt rather than to resolve it.

Eiran answered every question. He did not raise his voice, or become frustrated, nor let his patience be mistaken for condescension. Though he would have, in Seraphine's opinion, been entitled to it. He continued with the steady, unhurried certainty of someone who knew that they were right because the data proved it.

A junior scholar in the second row asked a genuine question about future expedition parameters, what other data needed to be gathered. Eiran's answer was longer, more specific, and a few fae near the front leaned forward.

At the back of the room, Seraphine's hands shook with fury.

She wasn't angry at anything that had been directly said, but at the performance of authority by fae whose command had calcified into something that no longer required effort or accuracy to sustain itself. They were right, or believed themselves to be, because no one had challenged them on it. It was apparent in their dismissal of data that threatened the comfort of their positions. The folded arms and close-mindedness of those who couldn't be bothered to consult the appendix. It was one thing to be stubborn and right, but it was unacceptable to ignore facts for the sake of preserving what was familiar.

Eiran had spent three years on his research, and the man in the third row would return home with his position intact and his arms folded, his copy of the papers unread and his institution's inertia undisturbed. Eiran would come back next year with more data, and the man would fold his arms again.

Seraphine was still furious when she met Eiran outside afterward.

He came through the lecture hall doors and found her one the steps. One look at her face, and he stopped.

"The Halveth surveys," she said.

He tugged on the bottom of his jacket, straightening it. "Are forty years old and methodology limited, yes."

"He didn't open the appendix."

Eiran gave her a sad sort of smile. "And he probably won't ever open it."

"Then what was the point of putting it in there in the first place?"

"For the people who will," he said simply. He stood beside her on the steps, looking out at the university's central courtyard, the evening light turning the stonework a shade of brilliant amber. "Aldric won't be moved. He's sat in that same seat for thirty years while the corruption has been a distant, theoretical problem for all of them. His career is built on a body of work that my data complicates. I'm not going to change his mind in a lecture hall."

"Then why—"

"Because the woman, the junior scholar, who asked the good questions will go back to her office and read the appendix. Then read the methodology and run the numbers herself." Eiran shot Seraphine a sidelong glance. "In three years, she'll have data of her own. Aldric will retire, and the room will be different."

Seraphine's hands had stilled, but the anger still pulsed beneath her skin like molten metal. Eiran was entirely serious and calm in a way she found difficult to match.

"You're not angry," she said.

"No."

"How?" She couldn't fathom his calm. If anyone had questioned her that way, in response to data that was clear as glass, she wouldn't be so composed.

He considered her question. "Because being angry at Aldric would require me to have expected something different from him. And I know Aldric." He fingered one of the buttons on his jacket. "Are you angry at the alloy when it doesn't behave the way an inferior grade would?"

"That is not the same thing," Seraphine said.

He gave her a rueful smile. "It's a little the same."

She looked away. A moment passed between them. She felt his hand find hers, brief and light. His warm fingers enveloped her own.

"It means something to me. That you're upset." He kept his hand on hers.

Seraphine didn't answer. Eiran willed his wings away, no longer needed them. They walked to the workshop, their fingers still entwined.

Seraphine stopped at the door. "I want to ask you something," she said. "And I want you to understand that I have considered it carefully before asking, because I don't ask things I haven't considered carefully."

Eiran waited. He was good at waiting.

"You should move in. Here," she said. "The middle floor has more room than I use. Your books would fit. Your notebooks would fit." She paused. "You would fit."

The street was quiet around them, save for the slow sounds of water under the canal, lapping at the banks. He looked at her for a moment, in the way he studied things he was genuinely trying to understand.

She held his gaze and did not qualify what she had said or offer him an easier version of it. She had meant it. All she had now, was to wait for his response.

"You've been thinking about this for a while," he said.

"Yes."

"How long?"

She gave the accurate answer. "Since you reorganized my supply shelf."

He smiled slowly, as though he had she had just confirmed something he had already suspected for some time, and she was now confirming it. "That was four months ago," he said.

"I'm aware."

"Seraphine."

"I know it's —" she stopped. Started again, because she had said she would be honest and she intended to be. "I know it is not a small thing to ask. I'm not uncomplicated to live with. I work early and late and I have strong opinions about the organization of shelves."

"I know," he said. "I've reorganized several of them."

"You have." She looked at the door, then back at him. "The offer stands regardless of what you decide. I wanted you to know that I was asking because I wanted to, not because I thought I should. There is a difference."

He closed the distance between them and put his hand against her face, his thumb at her cheekbone.

Her breath caught, despite herself.

"Yes," he said. "May I kiss you?"

She opened her mouth to speak but found that she had no words. So, she nodded instead.

His lips pressed against hers, softly, tentatively, then with an urgency that surprised Seraphine. What surprised her more was that she matched his intensity. She placed her hands over his chest, feeling the rough texture of the borrowed jacket.

Eiran placed his hand at the small of her back and pulled her impossibly close.

After a moment, they pulled apart, seeming to realize at the same time that they were still outside. Seraphine opened the door, their door, and Eiran followed her upstairs. She left the door open for him while she went upstairs and stood at the workshop window for a moment, looking at the canal below and the moonlight on the water. She heard him on the stairs, and then he was in the workshop doorway, the green coat over his arm, his notebook already set on the chair by the window as though it had always lived there.

She turned from the window.

Eiran's eyes were dark and searching. Seraphine recognized the sparks in the air between them. It felt like the moment just before a binding sealed, when everything that needed to happen had been decided. The only thing that remained was simply the completion of it. Certainty swelled in her chest. As if she had finally arrived at a place she'd been moving toward for a long time. She crossed the workshop and Eiran set his coat down.

LATER, Seraphine lay in the dark with the canal sounds coming through the open window and his breathing slow and even beside her. She thought about the supply shelf, and the chair by the window, and all the small ordinary ways a person could become so ingrained in your life without your noticing until they already were.

She had noticed, she thought sleepily. She had simply taken four months to say so.

EIRAN WAS INVITED as a presenting scholar to the council function three weeks later. A formal reception in one of the civic buildings near the government quarter. The function was held on a building that was all pale stone and high ceilings.

Seraphine came because Eiran asked her and because she had learned, over the past months, that his reasons for asking were usually worth attending to.

Councilor Valdris found them within twenty minutes of their arrival.

He was late middle age for a fae, the kind of silver-haired authority that Grauradur produced in quantity. His appearance was well-maintained and comfortable in the way of those who had spent their careers in rooms exactly like this one. His wings were large and white, a symbol of his power and authority within the council.

Valdris moved through the reception with practiced ease, something he had clearly perfected as a practical skill. He stopped at each group long enough to make the stop feel significant and left before the conversation became an obligation. Wherever he moved, a small gust followed.

He reached them and extended his hand to Eiran with a warmth that was equally as well-executed.

"Your symposium has been the talk of the university. Thank you for coming. The boundary data is remarkable. The council has been following your work with considerable interest."

"I'm glad it's reached you," Eiran said.

"Reached us? We've been waiting for it." Valdris turned to Seraphine with the same warmth, redirected seamlessly. "And you must be the artificer. Eiran speaks highly of your work. The Thaumic Meridian is inspired, from what I understand."

"It does what the commission required," Seraphine said.

He smiled at that. It was genuine-seeming, appreciative of the deflection without being destabilized by it. She watched him the way she watched materials she hadn't worked with before, reading the surface for what lay underneath. He was warm and engaged. He said the right things about Eiran's research and the council's commitment to addressing the corruption threat and the importance of rigorous data in policy formation.

All of it was true, as far as she could tell. But that was not what bothered her.

There was a gap between his warmth and the thing underneath it. It was not coldness exactly, or malice. She couldn't have said precisely what was missing. Only that something was, in the way she could tell a piece had a flaw before she'd identified where. Seraphine filed this information about Valdris away.

Valdris moved on with the fluid grace of someone who had many fae to speak to and wanted each of them to feel they'd been given his full attention.

Seraphine watched him cross the room.

"What are you thinking about?" Eiran asked beside her.

Seraphine continued to study Valdris across the reception, who was currently bestowing his warmth on a senior faculty member she recognized from the symposium. "He's going to commission your expedition," she said. As she spoke the words aloud, an odd tension settled in her stomach.

Eiran followed her gaze. "That's rather the hope."

"I know." She picked up her glass and took a sip.

THE COMMISSION CAME six days later, delivered by formal letter to Eiran's office at the university. He brought it to the workshop, his steps quicker than usual, his coat and hair damp from the light rain outside. He set the letter on the bench in front of her without sitting down in his chair first.

Seraphine read the letter, printed on thick paper. The terms were to assess the southern boundary regions for three months with three accompanying scholars. There was a formal risk assessment provided by the council's advisory board, documentation requirements, and the stipulation that a report be completed within thirty days upon return.

The risk assessment was four pages and cited the Halveth surveys.

She set the packet down. "Their threshold estimates are based on methodology you've already demonstrated is insufficient." She suddenly felt cold. It was raining, yes, but it was not overly chilly outside.

"Which is why the expedition is necessary," Eiran said. He studied her, and spoke with care, knowing that this conversation had two layers and both needed navigating. "The risk assessment is conservative. The council—"

"Used the Halveth surveys."

"Seraphine."

She looked at the letter on the bench, then at him. His eyes were bright. A vibrant energy radiated from him. After three years, his work was finally moving from theory to the field. She knew what it meant, and that she could not say exactly what she was thinking. It was not about his judgement, but her fear, and she didn't want to dim the light in his eyes.

So, she got up and put the kettle on over the forge's flame, which she made gentle with a soft command of her magic. "When do they need an answer?"

Eiran still had not moved to his chair. "End of the week."

She made the tea. She set his cup in front him on the bench. She held her own cup between her hands and looked at the letter between them.

He was going to go. She knew this with certainty. The letter was only a formality. His decision had been made during months of data collection, in reading reports and writing them, in presenting at the symposium, and when they'd walked home with their fingers entwined. She'd known it then.

Seraphine drank her tea and did not say what she was thinking. That the Halveth surveys were forty years old, methodologically limited, and the man who had written the risk assessment had not, she was almost certain, ever opened Eiran's appendix.

"It's a good opportunity," she said, lowering her cup.

"It is."

Outside the rain came down harder against the open windows. Neither of them left to fetch the towel for the workbench.

CHAPTER

# NINE

Eiran signed the commission at the end of the week, then told Seraphine two days later. He had given himself two whole days with it before telling her.

Seraphine noted this without saying anything. She took it to mean he had wanted to be certain before the conversation, which meant he had known it would be difficult. It also meant he had been paying attention, which she didn't fault him for, even though she wanted to.

He came in the evening with a fresh-baked loaf of bread from the market and let himself in with the key she had given him after the colloquium. Eiran made dinner downstairs as she finished the piece she was working on. Then she closed the windows and banked the forge for the night.

She joined him downstairs when she was finished, and they ate together at the kitchen table. They shared their meal in comfortable, companionable quiet. It wasn't until Seraphine was washing up that Eiran said from the table behind her, "I signed it yesterday."

69

Seraphine kept the water running, kept scrubbing the plates.

"We're leaving in four weeks."

She shut off the water, set the final dish in the drying rack, and turned around.

Eiran's eyes were pinched at the corners, as if he were bracing himself.

Seraphine was not ready to arrive at the end of something she hadn't even started arguing yet. "Four weeks."

"The window for safe passage through the southern pass is limited. If we don't go in four weeks, we must wait another six months."

"Then wait."

"Seraphine—"

She moved to the table and placed herself across from him, but she did not sit. "The risk assessment cites the Halveth surveys. The council used them to assess the risk of an expedition into the exact region your data shows has degraded beyond what the surveys could detect." She held his gaze and pressed her palms flat on the table. "They are sending you in with the wrong numbers. You know they are doing so *with the wrong numbers.*"

"The surveys are limited. That's why I'm going. To replace them with accurate data. If what I suspect is true, then the corruption is spreading. Slowly, but it's moving. If we have accurate information, we can act accordingly. Plan to mitigate any threat before it becomes a problem."

"What if you push back on the timeline. Ask them to commission an updated risk assessment before you depart." Seraphine's hands tingled again like sparks in a forge.

He tapped a long finger on the table. "From whom? I'm the only researcher with current boundary data. The updated risk assessment would require the expedition to complete."

Seraphine straightened and flexed her fingers. "Then ask for more support. Another scholar with field experience, a larger party. Something that accounts for the gap between the risk assessment says and what your data suggests."

"The support is adequate as it stands, and for what I expect to encounter."

Keeping her voice even required effort. "You said it yourself at the symposium. Remote mapping can't see everything. That's the argument you made for going in the first place."

"Yes, and it's still true. Which is why I have to go."

"It is not the only reason you have to go. You have chosen to go, and those are different things."

Eiran was quiet for a moment. When he spoke again, his voice shifted into a tone that was more serious than she had ever heard him use.

"You're right. I have chosen it. I could push back on the timeline or spend six months negotiating the terms of the contract. I could wait for another window, or another after that. But the corruption doesn't wait."

His eyes hardened. He wasn't angry, but he understood the facts and the data, and his resolve had been made by them. "It has been spreading for the entirety of my career, and it will keep spreading while I'm negotiating the terms of the expedition that might produce data that would convince the council that it's a real problem. Fae are living in Tenebris, being consumed by something I have three years of data on, and no one in a position to act on it has seen it."

He sighed deeply. "The risk of going is less than the risk of no one going. I have weighed both options."

"You weighed them without telling me you were."

"I'm telling you now."

"You signed the commission first." Seraphine's eyes pricked with unshed tears. She refused to let them fall.

Hurt flashed across Eiran's face. "Yes, I did. Because I knew what I was going to decide and I didn't want the conversation to be about changing my mind. I wanted to tell you, not ask you. I should have told you before I signed. That was wrong, and I'm sorry for it."

The apology was genuine, but it did not heal the ache that had opened in her chest. "You're going regardless of what I say."

Eiran stood and moved around the table, cutting the distance between them. Light from the oil lamp made his whole face glow. "I'm going because I believe it's necessary. Not regardless of you. Those aren't the same thing. What you think matters to me. The fear you have for this—" He stopped, choosing his words carefully. "I know what it means that you're afraid. You don't frighten easily, and when you do, you don't say so. The fact that you raise these concerns tells me that you are afraid."

"And yet," she said. Her voice was so small.

"And yet."

Seraphine's hands trembled with the ember-spark feeling and her stomach clenched. Her mouth would not form the words she longed to say. She didn't know how to voice the tumultuous feelings inside of her body, ones that felt too foreign and overwhelming. Feelings she could not reason her way out of or make them fit neatly inside a table.

Eiran's face softened as she struggled. He tucked an errant strand of her white-blonde hair behind her ear. "I love you, Seraphine. I love you, and I'm going, and I cannot make those two things not true at the same time."

All the air vanished from the kitchen, like a flame that had been suddenly snuffed out. She had known, deep down. The rhythm of their days spent together, the fact that she had given him a key and always set out two cups of tea. Of course she had known he loved her, but they had not spoken of it until now. And he had chosen now, and she could not decide if that was brave or terrible.

Seraphine fought to make her lungs, her lips, work. "That is a very inconvenient time to say that."

Eiran gave her a rueful smile. "I'm sorry." But he didn't look sorry at all. He looked relieved, like he had been waiting to say it for a long, long time. "I've been trying to find a better moment for months. There wasn't one."

"I love you, too," she said without embellishment, because it was true and true things deserved to be said plainly. "I have loved you for long enough that I can't identify the beginning of it, which is not a condition I am accustomed to, and it is alarming. When I say the risk assessment is insufficient—" her voice broke. She cleared her throat and started again. "I'm saying it as someone who has read the surveys and as someone who needs you to come back."

Eiran pulled her against his chest and buried his face into the top of her head. "I intend to," he said, his voice muffled.

Seraphine let herself melt into him, cherishing the closeness, letting the warmth of his body chase away the chill inside her.

He shifted, just enough to look into her eyes. "I will come back and tell you I was right about the data and argue with you about it for the rest of what I expect to be a very long life."

Seraphine smiled despite the tears that now dripped freely down her face. "You will not be right about the data. You will simply have more of it, which is different."

"I'll be right about what the data means."

"You will have an interpretation of it, which I will find several problems with."

"Undoubtedly." He stroked his thumb across her cheek, wiping away her tears. "Seraphine. I am coming back."

She believed him with the full weight of everything she knew about him. His patience, three years of careful work, the composure she found both admirable and maddening that was not indifference but a settled relationship with the truth of things. He believed he was coming back. He would do everything in his power to make that true.

Seraphine also knew that the corruption didn't care what he intended. She'd heard the stories, same as everyone. She liked to think she was above the fear that came with them. But most stories about the corruption were based in fact. She was an artificer, who made items of use for merchants, travelers, and traders. And the owner of the compass who had requested a recalibration but never returned to collect it had been traveling to the southern pass. There were some folk who did not return, and it was glaringly obvious what had happened to them.

"Let's go to bed," she said. It was late, and she was tired, felt things at full volume for an extended period of time.

Eiran raised his eyebrows.

"Please," Seraphine whispered.

He nodded and followed her into her bedchamber.

They lay in the dark and in the silence that was left after

an argument. All the things that had been said, and left unsaid, hung in the air between them. The city outside eventually grew quiet. Indigo night swept over Grauradur, and stars blazed to life in the sky.

His hand found hers in the dark.

She let her hand stay under his for a few heartbeats. Then she slid closer to him, placing her hand on his chest, her mouth on his, craving him. The ache in her chest could only be soothed by holding him as close as possible.

Seraphine moaned softly as he trailed kisses down her neck and ran his hands over her, as desperate for contact as she was.

She loved him. She could not make him stay. She had known before the argument began. Perhaps since the first time he'd mentioned the idea of an expedition, and she had changed the subject rather than examine what his leaving would mean.

"I love you," she whispered, trailing her fingers over his cheekbone, through his tousled hair.

He kissed her deeply. Both his forearms braced rested either side of her head, holding himself up above her. As their bodies moved in rhythm together, he whispered it back. "I love you, too."

A deep, soul-wracking pulse jumped between them, sealing their bond. They had chosen one another, and the magic that united their souls felt like sparks.

They did not sleep until the light began is slow, pale climb toward morning.

# TEN

Four weeks slipped by quickly, the way time moves when it's being watched with the hope that the hours will pass slowly, or not at all. Each day was now countable in a way ordinary days were not, heavy with the knowledge of how many remained.

Seraphine finished a resonance compass for a surveying firm. It was mid-complexity work, the kind she could complete in six days when her mind was fully tuned to the task. It took her ten. She checked it twice more than was necessary, found nothing wrong either time and packed it for delivery with flat efficiency.

Eiran finished his paper on boundary permeability, writing the final section one evening at their kitchen table. His notes spread across the table and two chairs. He read the conclusion aloud to her while she made dinner.

She had grown used to hearing the tenor of his voice fill the silence. She made to two corrections without turning from the stove. He incorporated both without argument, which meant he agreed with them. Eiran submitted the paper to the university's research journal the following morning.

The journal's acceptance arrived four days before his departure. Seraphine found it on the kitchen table when she came downstairs, already open. Eiran left it there with a cup of tea gone cold beside it. Seraphine set the letter back on the table, climbed the stairs to the workshop, and did not mention it until Eiran arrived that evening to join her for dinner.

She said it was good news, and he agreed. They spoke of other, idle things because there was not much space in those last few days for the full weight of all they felt.

THE NEXT MORNING, he relabeled her supply jars. He stationed himself on the east wall with a pot of ink and a pen, transferring her labels onto new paper in his own handwriting. His script was neat and slanted to the left. It was efficiently legible, if not elegant. He was on the jar of copper filings when she came up from the lower level, having already done the iron powder, silver dust, and resonance salts.

She stood in the doorway and watched him, holding two cups of tea.

"The paper on these jars are starting to lift at the corners," he said without turning around. "In another year they'll be completely illegible."

"I know what's in the jars," Seraphine said.

"You do. Your apprentice, when you take one, will not."

Seraphine didn't have an apprentice. She had declined

three guild referrals in the past decade on the grounds that she worked better alone. Eiran knew this. Seraphine looked at the jars he'd already done, his handwriting on her shelves, the labels straight and neat.

"You're not going to comment on how the humidity of the room is certainly to blame for the deterioration of my labels?"

He turned to look at her then, with one brow raised. "I believe you already know my stance on your window habits."

Seraphine set his cup down on the window ledge for him. A soft summer breeze that smelled of rich, growing things and cool water, wafted into the workshop. "I do."

She went back to the bench and did not tell him to stop. There were perhaps a dozen small tasks he should be completing at this moment. His expedition was leaving in mere days. Yet he chose to spend his time labeling her jars of materials.

When Eiran finished he put the ink away in the correct drawer, washed the pen in the basin, and sat in his chair. He picked up his book and read while she worked. The afternoon wore on, and she did not look at the shelf until he had gone home for the evening. There was, he admitted, much to do. Eiran promised to be back early the next morning.

In his absence, Seraphine studied his handwriting on every jar. She left them exactly as he'd done them.

～

ON THE MORNING of his departure, Eiran left his book face-down on the windowsill. He had been reading it the evening before, their last evening they'd spend together for three months, and he set it there as he always did: spine up, pages open. It was still there in the morning because he has come upstairs already packed, moving with focused energy.

Seraphine had woken far earlier than usual, unable to sleep. She stood at her workbench, wrestling with a technical problem she had been turning over for three days. A question of alloy composition for a commission she hadn't started yet. The problem was genuinely demanding enough that her mind was occupied, which she was grateful for.

Eiran came upstairs, and she looked up.

He was dressed for travel. He wore his green coat, and his satchel was slung over his shoulder. His expedition pack sat by the door, waiting for him to collect it.

"The supply cart leaves from the university at eight," he said. "I need to go."

Seraphine set down her tools. She let her gaze linger on the milk jug at the end of the bench before her eyes found his.

There was too much to say. She let herself note also, for the briefest second, how much had changed since she'd first received his letter requesting a commission months ago. How she had slowly, softly, allowed him into her life. Had let him weave himself into the texture of her days.

She blinked, and said, "The secondary calibration ring. Counter-clockwise to slow the pulse. Don't let the other scholars touch the frequency settings without you present."

"I know."

"The alloy will tarnish after in high-corruption environments. Check it weekly."

"I will."

He let his satchel fall from his shoulder and moved across the room to her. Eiran placed his hands on either side of her face. He kissed her, thorough and unhurried, in the way he did most things. He pressed his forehead to hers.

Seraphine's hands found the front of his coat. She gripped so tightly her knuckles turned white.

"I'll write when we're through the pass."

"Thank you," she said.

He kissed her again, and she let herself fall into his scent, his warmth.

Eventually she released him, because she had to.

Eiran picked up his pack and went down the stairs. She heard the street door, then his footsteps on the cobblestones, then the city took him and there were only the ambient sounds of waking streets, the canal, the fae on their way to the market. The bright, relentless light of Grauradur streamed in through the open windows.

Seraphine took up her place at her bench again. She had not, in that goodbye, told him she loved him. They had shared those words in the kitchen and in her bedroom, and Eiran knew that she did. There would be time to tell him again when he returned.

THE FIRST LETTER arrived eleven days later, confirming that Eiran had made it safely through the Durnath, the mountain pass on the southern border.

He wrote her four pages that were dense with observation, his handwriting a little sloppier than usual, as if he'd written in haste. The journey through the pass took two days and had been, he wrote, extraordinary in its geological complexity. The rock revealed a history of magical and tectonic activity that warranted its own study. Tenebris had exceeded his expectations in every manner. The corruption at the boundary was measurable and consistent with the remote data he'd been able to gather over the past three years. This was extremely gratifying, and the Thaumic Meridian was performing within all specified parameters. The ambient magical interference in the first survey zone was within the tolerance range she had designed for. His colleagues, the assigned research staff, were competent. The weather was cool and clear.

At the bottom of the page, in smaller writing than the rest, he'd added: *The coat is holding up. I told you it had more in it.*

Seraphine read the letter twice. She placed it at the top of her bench, within view of her periphery as she worked. She returned to her commission.

She received another letter eight days after the first. This one was six pages, and Eiran shared again in hasty, near-breathless sentences, that the corruption gradient in the deeper survey zones was more complex than the remote mapping had suggested. He wrote about it with fascination rather than concern. He had three new hypotheses which he briefly outlined, and she could see they would expand into perhaps three new papers upon his return. The Thaumic Meridian had required one minor recalibration. The secondary ring, counterclockwise, exactly has she'd specified.

The third letter came a week and a half after the second. It was shorter than the others, the handwriting less smudged and slanted. The deeper zones required more time than scheduled. The corruption patterns at the boundary between the second and third survey zones were unlike anything that existed in literature or the Halveth surveys.

Eiran was extending the survey period by two weeks. He was well. The Meridian was functioning properly, just as she'd designed. He'd begun revising his journal paper, integrating his new findings and data.

*The corruption is fascinating up close. It isn't frightening. It's more like watching the weather than anything malicious. I keep wondering what you would make of it. I think you would find it interesting despite yourself.*

Seraphine let her fingers linger on that last paragraph.

She did not receive a fourth letter.

THE POSTAL ROUTE through the Durnath Pass was unreliable. Seraphine told herself this repeatedly because it was true. She also told herself the extended survey timeline had taken him further from relay points, that he was occupied with the data, that letter-writing was secondary to the work, and that he would write when he had something worth reporting.

For twenty-one days she told herself these things, shoving aside the sensation of *wrongness* that plagued her, that corroded her insides and ate away at the space that had so recently been filled with her connection to him. A light had gone dark, but she refused to see it.

On the twenty-second day she heard footsteps on the stairs she didn't recognize. Two sets, heavier than Eiran's tread. She knew before the knock.

Two scholars were at her door. She recognized one of them from the symposium. They had the careful expressions of people who had prepared what they were going say and were hoping their preparation would be sufficient.

It wasn't.

They told her that the expedition had reached the third zone. That the corruption there had advanced beyond the mapped boundaries, further and faster than the risk assessment had accounted for, and that the mist in the third zone was not simply weather. It took Eiran before anyone understood what was happening, and by the time they realized, there was nothing to be done and nothing to bring back. They told her he had not suffered. It was quick. More like sleep than anything else.

Seraphine heard what they told her. She thanked them, then she closed the door and stood with her back against it for a moment. Her hand remained on the latch. The workshop was the same as it had been minutes ago. It was also entirely different. The light through the open windows streamed in as it always did, indifferent to the fact that everything had shifted.

She sat down at her bench. Seraphine stayed there until the light changed, then it was gone and the room was dark. She did not move to light the lamp.

THE KETTLE BOILED. She was at the bench before she was fully awake, her body knowing the room and the routine before her mind had arrived to supervise. The whistle pierced the silence. She took the kettle from the heat and set out two cups.

She stood there as pale grey light bloomed into the workshop with a kettle in one hand and two cups set before her. The milk just sat at the end of her bench where it always was. His handwriting on the labels of the eastern shelf. His book still face-down on the windowsill where he had left it seven weeks ago. The city moved below the window. Water rushed in the canal.

She put the kettle down and stood there a little while longer with the two cups in front of her. Steam rose from one of them, but not the other.

CHAPTER

# ELEVEN

The guild sent three commissions in the first month. Small ones, the kind that required competence rather than attention. Seraphine completed them. The clients received what they paid for and left satisfied. She took two more and completed those, too. The first month passed.

She did not move his book.

It remained face-down on the windowsill all through the fall and winter. The pages softened in the damp air, the spine curved from being held open so long. She knew which book it was. She had opinions about it, about the argument its author made that she had told Eiran was structurally unsound. He had disagreed with her on grounds that were still insufficient. She did not close the book or read it. She left it exactly where it was, open to the page he had been reading.

She kept his letters on the workbench. Seraphine had read them enough times that she did not need to unfold them to know what they said. She unfolded them anyway most evenings. They had gone soft at the creases from her handling, the fibers separating where the paper had been folded and unfolded too many times. She was aware that she was damaging it. She could not stop.

She moved through commissions mechanically. A warding matrix, a set of locating charms, two navigation instruments for a cartography firm that contracted regularly with the guild. The work was technically sound. Her clients did not complain.

Seraphine understood that the work was not what it had been, that something in her had gone flat, but she could not locate the specific mechanism of the flatness.

She did not cry. Grief was not a single thing.

THREE MONTHS after Seraphine was told about Eiran, when ice and snow had descended in full on Grauradur, the university sent a notice that his office and research materials required clearing out. The department had held them as long as procedurally permissible under the faculty research retention policy, which allowed ninety days for estates or designated persons to claim academic materials before they were archived or redistributed.

She had not known that Eiran named her as an authorized person to collect his research. Seraphine went early in the week, on the day Eiran had first started coming to the workshop to check on his commission. Her body expected something to happen on these days, and she found it was better to give it something than to leave it expecting.

The department's administrative assistant, a precise older woman named Corva, managed the research faculty's paperwork with the philosophy that proper filing was a form of respect. Corva met her at the office door with a signed release form and neutrality that Seraphine recognized as professional kindness. The assistant unlocked the office, showed her the inventory list of materials, and told her she could have the afternoon.

Eiran's office was small, with one south-facing window that looked into the university's inner courtyard where a fountain splashed in its center. He had arranged his office in a manner that made sense to him and probably made very little sense to anyone else. Seraphine, having watched him organize the spices in her kitchen, label the jars in her workshop, and attempt to relocate her copper filings, understood. Books were organized by a sequence that informed each other, rather than by author or title. Survey maps pinned to the wall in geographical order, annotated in his handwriting. Three years of field notebooks stacked on the leftmost bookshelf, labeled by date and survey zone in the slanted writing she knew better than her own.

The filter she had made him lay on the corner of his desk. The small oval of resonance alloy in its plain wire mount, set to the side where it was visible but not in the way. The wire had begun to tarnish. She had told him to bring it back to her when he did.

She stood in the center of the office. The room still smelled like him. She picked up the resonance filter and put it in her coat pocket and felt the chasm of emptiness inside herself.

Seraphine did not take the books or the maps. Those

belonged to the department, to the next researcher. She took all his field notebooks, stacking them carefully into the crate she'd brought. She took the draft of his boundary permeability paper, too. Then she sat in his chair.

It was plain and wooden, standard university issue. Where many scholars might have brought in a more comfortable seat, replacing the stiff standard-issue, he had not. She sat in the chair and looked at the desk from where he had looked at it. On the cleared surface, a square of afternoon light on the wood. The courtyard outside where a woman crossed with her arms full of documents and her head bowed against the wind.

Seraphine sat there for five or so minutes. She did not know how long exactly, as she wasn't measuring.

Finally, she made herself stand up. She settled the crate on her hip, signed the release form on her way out and thanked Corva. The assistant nodded with the same professional neutrality and did not ask what she had taken.

THAT EVENING she set one of his notebooks beside her tools on the workbench. She didn't open it. The work she was doing required both hands and most of her attention. Besides, she wasn't ready to open it. She set it there because the process of clearing out his things from his office had made his absence concrete. Keeping the notebook there at her workspace, as he had kept the resonance filter on his own desk, made him feel near in the only way available.

The lamplight added a warm, golden glow to the workshop. The canal moved sluggishly below the window, slowed by the ice on its banks. Someone on the bridge laughed, the sound carrying in the cold air.

Seraphine worked. The notebook sat beside her tools, Eiran's handwriting on the cover, the dates of the first survey zone. She was not ready to read it yet, but she was glad it was there.

CHAPTER

# TWELVE

Three measured raps knocked on the workshop door the following week. Seraphine had not recognized the tread on the stairs. She opened the door.

The fae on the landing was perhaps a decade younger than Seraphine, with dark hair and dressed in the sleek charcoal grey robes of a junior council representative. She carried no portfolio, guild notice, or any apparatus that typically preceded an official council visit. She held her pointed chin high, but there was nothing overly stiff in her posture. She looked at Seraphine directly, without the practiced warmth council representatives usually deployed at first meetings.

She said, "My name is Mira Aster. I'm a junior representative in the council's advisory division. I wanted to come before the others, if you'll allow it."

Seraphine studied her for a moment. *Before the others.* She made a mental note and stood aside.

The woman came in and looked at the workshop with curiosity, taking inventory without trying to appear she was doing so. Her eyes moved across the bench, the tools, the forge in the corner, the shelf with the labeled jars, the open window. She did not comment on any of it.

"Sit down," Seraphine said. She put the kettle on, lowering the flame of the forge before she did so with barely a thought. Seraphine made tea because it was something to do with her hands, and it established the terms of the visit without requiring either of them to negotiate them. A cup of tea was not an invitation to stay indefinitely but it provided a reasonably long enough interval to conduct whatever business this woman had brought.

Mira did not attempt to fill the silence, which Seraphine appreciated.

The kettle boiled, and Seraphine removed it from the fire, letting the flames return to a moderate height, warming the workshop. She set the cups down and sat across from Mira.

"You don't know me. I should say that straightaway, since I am coming to you without introduction."

"You've introduced yourself."

"I've given my name. That's not the same thing." She took a delicate sip of her tea. Her chin-length hair swung forward, curtaining her face. "I've been a junior representative in the advisory division for six years. My work is primarily in policy research, which means I read a great deal of documentation that other people summarize before it reaches the senior council. I'm telling you this because it's relevant to why I'm here. I'd rather you understand my position clearly, rather than have to infer it."

Seraphine wrapped her hands around her mug, letting the warmth sink into her fingers. "All right."

"I knew Eiran. Not well. We spoke at a council reception, and he said something about boundary permeability data that I've found myself thinking about since."

Mira paused briefly, deliberately. "I sent a condolence letter."

The warmth left Seraphine's hands, even though they were still wrapped around the mug of hot tea. "It reached me. I remember it."

Mira's posture settled. She hadn't known whether the letter had been received the way she'd intended it. Seraphine added this detail to the developing picture of the fae across from her. A person who cared how a condolence letter was received might be a person worth listening to.

"The council will be sending a formal delegation to your workshop within a fortnight. Councilor Aldaveth will lead it. There may be others, but I wanted you to know before they arrived."

"Why?"

"There are questions you should ask that the delegation will not volunteer the answer to. It's easier to prepare questions when you've had time to think."

Seraphine released her mug. "What does the council want?"

"An artificer. The best artificer, actually. The corruption spread in the southern regions has become impossible to defer politically. Three boundary incidents in the pass in the past year. The surveys are indicating acceleration." She said the last slowly, carefully choosing her words.

"How much acceleration?"

"That is a question for the delegation."

Seraphine kept her gaze fixed firmly on Mira.

The junior councilor dropped her almond-shaped eyes to the table, her tea, before looking up once more. "The council's official position references the Halveth surveys as the baseline assessment."

Seraphine knew this. "Their methodology has been formally contested. Eiran's research demonstrated their resolution was insufficient for accurate gradient mapping."

"Yes. I'd ask the delegation for the full surveying reports. Not the summary. The *complete* reports. I would also ask what the specific acceleration figures show, and over what period they were recorded."

"The delegation will answer these questions?"

"I expect they will answer the questions they are prepared to. I wanted to...*suggest* which questions might be beneficial to you."

Seraphine understood what Mira was doing. The woman across from her, Mira, had worked in her role for six years, reading documentation that other summarized. She clearly knew the difference between an official position and fact. "You have concerns," Seraphine said.

"Nothing that I can substantiate to an evidentiary standard."

"About the acceleration data specifically."

Mira tucked her hair behind a slender, pointed ear. "About several things. I've sat in a great many meetings and learned to notice when the summary position and the attitude of the people of the room do not exactly match."

Seraphine found herself looking over at Eiran's note book, lying next to her tools on the bench. She thought about his letters. About the gradient maps in the third survey zone, his change in his handwriting as the readings got stranger. Her mind worried over the risk assessment the council had provided, snagging on it like a sharp corner of alloy that needed filing. And the damned Halveth surveys and the man at the symposium who had not opened the appendix.

"What do they want made?"

"They're not sure. They understand that magic can act as a counterforce to corruption, but there is nothing on record specific enough to constitute a technical brief. They need an artificer who is skilled and has studied the corruption, rather than someone who has only studied the theory of counterforce. Someone with the right knowledge." Mira swallowed before she continued. "And the right motive. You are the only person they're considering."

The only person. Seraphine tucked this away, too, in case she might have need of it. "I'd want full access to their archives," she said. "Not the summary documents. Everything filed under pre-council reference on corruption, counterforce theory, old artificer texts, and full surveying reports."

Mira gave her a small smile. "That's exactly what I'd ask for."

Seraphine took another sip of her tea. It had cooled just enough to be annoyingly tepid. "I haven't agreed to anything."

Mira reached into her coat and produced a single sheet of folded paper and set it on the table between them. "I copied this from the archive index. The full document is held under a pre-council reference code in a restricted section. The delegation will bring a summary only. You should read the full document."

Seraphine beheld the paper between them without touching it. Reaching for it felt more like a commitment than she was ready to make. But her curiosity, her need to fill in the tables of missing information, won out. She read the paper twice, the way she read anything of importance.

She thought about refusing. She had been managing her

commissions and the weight of the past months. What Mira was describing would take more than simple management. This was the kind of work that would pull everything she had out of her, then ask for more. She was not sure she had anything left to give.

Eiran's notebook caught her attention again. He had found the corruption fascinating, instead of fearing it. Perhaps he should have. He had never been able to resist the pull of something he found fascinating, and so he'd gone into the third survey zone and found data that was abnormal.

*The risk of going is less than the risk of no one going.*

That was what he had said.

Something in her cracked open, like a pale beam of light breaking through an overcast day.

"Can you get me full archive access, in writing, before the delegation arrives? Not verbal assurance. A formal document from the council's records division. Notarized."

Mira nodded once. "I'll see what I can do."

"And the full survey reports. Every single one," Seraphine added.

"Those will require the delegation's formal authorization. Ask for them in the meeting. In writing."

"I will." Seraphine sipped her tea even though it was cold. "Thank you for coming, Mira Aster."

Mira stood and gathered her coat. At the door she paused, her hand on the frame. "When you are in the archive," she said, without turning around, "the restricted holdings are organized by council review period. The current period began eleven years ago. The collateral documentation category was introduced in the reform process fourteen years ago. It is used for materials that require formal filing but do not require prominent placement." She turned and looked at Seraphine with sharp directness that had been there from the beginning. "The reform process also introduced a provision requiring all survey materials related to active expedition commissions to be cross-referenced in the primary index."

Mira's footsteps faded down the stairs, light, even, and measured. The workshop settled back into stillness.

Seraphine eyed the paper Mira had left behind again as her mind churned over acceleration figures, the Halveth surveys, Eiran at her table, bright eyes and immovable. His hand over hers in the dark. Her thoughts then turned to what Mira had said.

Cross-referenced in the primary index. Which meant that if a survey report existed that should have been cross-referenced and was not, the absence of the cross-reference would itself be a record. A gap in the index where something should have been.

She was not looking for a document. She was looking for a missing document.

She moved to the bench and opened Eiran's notebook to the last entry. Seraphine read it once standing up. Then, she took a seat and read it again. She pulled her own notes toward her and began.

Four members of the delegation arrived at the end of the week. Seraphine recognized Aldaveth, who handled most of the guild's formal dealings with the council. He was a fae of considerable age, silver-haired with a heavily lined face. Two junior staff wearing gray robes, a man and a woman, carried thick portfolios and bore carefully neutral expressions that clearly communicated they were simply there to record the proceedings. And Valdris.

Seraphine had not seen him since the council reception fourteen months ago. That evening she had watching him move through the room, bestowing his warmth and attention like a carefully allocated resource. He had not changed since then. He wore a long silver chain, noting the rank of his office, and slate blue councilor robes. He scanned the workshop, eagle-eyed, and did not offer any comment on what he beheld. A small part of her was gratified to see that he was forced to will away his domineering wings in her workshop, the space intentionally designed to discourage fae from displaying them here.

Aldaveth, having dealt most with Seraphine, made the formal opening. The council offered their condolences on Eiran's passing. He outlined the council's commission with the thoroughness of someone who had rehearsed what they would say, noting the boundary incidents as one of many reasons why they were requesting her services.

Seraphine listened. A junior staff set a thick portfolio on her bench and opened it to the commission terms. She read them as Aldaveth spoke, as she preferred to verify what was being said matched what was printed on the page.

The timeline for their request was aggressive. The resource allocation was simply adequate, and the archive access was specified to be full restricted holdings, which meant that Mira had managed to grant her as much access as possible. Seraphine noted all of this with a neutral expression.

"What is it, exactly, that you want?"

"The corruption is spreading. We are looking for a way to prevent it from extending further, perhaps to nullify the effects. We believe you can employ the theory of counterbalance to great effect."

Seraphine flipped through the rest of the portfolio.

"We are aware," Aldaveth said after a pause, "that the parameters are ambitious. The council has full confidence that you are the right person for this work."

"That is rather an understatement," Valdris said from where he stood slightly apart from the others. "There is no one else in Caeledrath or Grauradur with your specific combination of skills and knowledge." He said it with the characteristic warmth he brought to everything. Genuine on the surface, but well-calibrated.

Seraphine eyed him warily, assessing him like she would materials she had not used before. She was surprised to see that he was, truly, sorry. Or at least he felt something akin to sorrow, that functioned like it. He bore a heaviness that he had not entirely succeeded in concealing. He had been the one to launch the expedition after all.

"I'll need every report filed in the past four years on the southern boundary corruption spread. The complete documents, with filing dates and reviewing councilors noted."

The delegation stilled. They had not prepared for this request. A junior staff looked to Aldaveth.

"Of course," he replied. "We'll have them sent from the records division within the week."

"I need access before I begin. Not concurrently."

"Understood."

"I would like the archive access to be active before you leave today. In writing, with the council's signatures of approval."

The other junior staff produced it from the second portfolio she clutched to her chest.

Seraphine accepted the document, signed her copy, and set it on the workbench. "I'll take the commission."

Aldaveth looked relived. The junior staff began gathering their documents with brisk efficiency. Valdris remained at the fringes, peering out the window.

She had agreed because the threat was real and the corruption was spreading. She had the capability and experience to make an object that could employ the counterbalance theory, and she had insight into Eiran's research that no other artificer could claim. These by themselves were good enough reasons for the council, but they were not Seraphine's only reasons for accepting.

The surveying reports would tell her what the council had known about the southern boundary zones and the corruption spread within them, and *when* they had known about it. The archive access would tell her what documentation existed on the expedition's risk assessment and who had reviewed it. The proximity to the fae who had commissioned Eiran's expedition would tell her things that documents couldn't, the kind of information that lived in pauses and careful word choices and the weight underneath practiced warmth.

Seraphine was going to find out exactly what had happened to Eiran.

Aldaveth concluded the formalities and shook her hand. The woman in gray robes gave Seraphine a copy of the signed commission terms, precisely ordered. Then the delegation moved to the door. All accept Valdris.

He stood in the doorway as the stairs creaked with the delegation's descent. "Vael would have been proud of you," Valdris said. "For taking this on."

Seraphine looked past the superficiality in his expression. The sincerity masked a heaviness, but she could make out nothing else. He was very good at being a councilor.

She held his gaze, keeping her face stoic. "Yes. He would have."

Valdris lingered a breath longer. Then he nodded once and left. His footsteps echoed in the stairwell. The door to the street opened, then closed, and the workshop was empty.

Seraphine stood at the bench. She read the signed

archive access document again, slowly this time, all the way to the bottom where the records division had stamped the paper with its formal seal. Then she set down the commission terms next to Eiran's notebook.

She had work to do.

CHAPTER

# FOURTEEN

The council's archive occupied the lowest two floors of a city council building in the government quarter. The buildings were older, but their white marble structures were kept polished and pristine. The canal that cut through this area was wider and slower. Stone bridges wide enough to fit six fae across spanned over it. Government officials, councilors, junior staff, and those who had business in this sector walked with purpose through the streets.

Seraphine had been inside the records building a handful of times. She remembered the cold stone floors and the stillness of rooms that held things no one had touched in a long time.

She arrived the morning after the delegation with her signed document of access and satchel of blank notebooks. Seraphine presented herself to the archivist on duty, a younger fae than she had dealt with on previous visits. He had wavy blonde hair that had been meticulously style, and his black and silver archivist robes were pressed. He reviewed her documentation with no small amount of skepticism. Access of this scope was, apparently, rare. Finding nothing strictly wrong with the signed and sealed document, he logged her access in the admissions register. Then, he assigned her to a reading room on the lowest floor and informed her that materials were requested by reference code at the main desk and would be delivered within thirty minutes of request by a courier enchantment. No materials were to leave the archives. She was permitted to take notes, but she was not permitted to make copies without a request, which took three working days to process.

Seraphine thanked him and went downstairs.

The reading room had one wooden table, two unforgiving wooden chairs, and a small desk light powered by weaker, older magic emitted a yellow glow. The lighting was merely adequate. Seraphine moved it to corner of the table and began with the reference codes Mira had given her.

The first three days she read everything available on the corruption itself. Most of the documents were old. Observational accounts from scholars who had studied Tenebris from a distance, theoretical frameworks built on incomplete data. The kind of work that accumulated over decades when the people doing it could not, or would not, get close enough to test their assumptions. Seraphine set those aside. Fear was not useful.

She did find a slim volume so old that the leather finding had dried to the texture of tree bark. The author was illegible, the title page water damaged. The text, however, was meticulous. Seraphine read and set the volume flat on the table and sit very still.

Corruption was not an opposing force to magic. It was magic that had become untethered from its source. From what had originally given it form and purpose. Unanchored, the magic did not disappear, it inverted. It became hungry the way anything does when it had been too long without what it needed. The corruption did not destroy because it was evil, or intentionally malicious. It destroyed because it was *lost*.

Seraphine read the passage again. She wrote it out in full in her notebook, word for word, because it was the first thing in the archive, she had read that felt true rather than observationally approximate.

She set down her pen and leaned back into the rigid chair, crossing her arms. Gooseflesh rippled up her skin, not just from the chill in the reading room. The corruption was a wound on the world that needed healing. It was spreading, consuming, trying aimlessly to fill itself with whatever it could reach. It was untethered from the thing that gave it structure and meaning.

Seraphine thought about Eiran's last letter. He'd called the corruption fascinating. More like watching the weather than anything malicious.

He'd been right. Eiran had gotten close enough to see it clearly. Nobody with the authority to act on his understanding of it had been listening.

She opened her notebook to a fresh page and began to sketch her ideas.

DURING THE NEXT FEW DAYS, Seraphine shifted her focus to counterbalance theory. The documents she requested were fragmentary, pulled from a half dozen different archival collections. None of them were comprehensive, each approaching the same principle from a different angle. The principle itself was consistent across all of them. Magic, when correctly anchored, could function as a stabilizing counterforce to corruption, which made even more sense since corruption was unanchored magic to begin with. The metaphors varied by author and tended to take certain liberties that were less scientific and more dramatic. A root system against erosion, a tuning fork bringing dissonance back into pitch, or a fixed point around which forces could be brought back into orbit.

The *how* was much less clear. What material would hold magic to function at such a scale? What did anchoring look like in practical terms, not theory?

Seraphine wrote for hours each day. The left side of her hand became stained with ink as her notebooks filled. Slowly, the picture assembled itself from the fragments. Each new piece revealing what else she needed to uncover. As those aspects became clear, she gained momentum in solving the puzzle. Each new bit of information told her where the adjacent pieces had to go.

She was not yet thinking about what she would build but outlining out the underlying logic of the problem in a framework she could understand. This was the proper order and which she had learned over twenty-two years of artificer work to trust.

Then, it was time to investigate what Mira Aster had told her to. Seraphine did not begin with the survey reports. She began with the primary index.

Mira had told her that survey materials related to active expedition commissions were required by the reform process to be cross-referenced there. Seraphine pulled the primary index for the period covering Eiran's expedition, reading it for what the pattern suggested should be there and was not.

It took two hours. The expedition commission was logged in the primary index under its council reference number, as expected. The risk assessment was cross-referenced, as expected. The expedition's formal report, submitted by the two surviving scholars on their return, was cross-referenced. Everything that should have been there was there.

Except the survey data.

An expedition commission of this type, crossing into an active corruption zone, required a current survey of the boundary conditions as part of its foundational documentation. The risk assessment cited the Halveth surveys, which were forty years old. For the Halveth surveys to be the current documentation, no newer survey of those boundary regions could have been formally filed in connection with this commission. But boundary surveys of the southern zones had been ongoing. She knew this from Eiran's own research, which referenced council-funded survey activity in the region up to eighteen months before his expedition departed. Those surveys had to be somewhere in the archive.

Seraphine requested the collateral documentation catalogue for the reform period via enchanted form and waited with her hands gripped together on top of the table. It arrived with a BANG in the reception slot of the reading room. The document was extensive. She worked through it methodically, the way she worked through anything that required patience rather than insight, category by category. Eventually, she found a filing reference in the third hour, tucked between a decommissioned equipment inventory and a series of geological survey appendices from a road construction project. The reference code was recent. The filing date was fourteen months before Eiran's expedition departed.

She requested the document. Valdris's signature was on the cover page. Review confirmed. Filed for record. No further action required at this time.

Seraphine spent forty minutes reading the report, because she read it slowly, carefully. Then she read it again. The data documented corruption spread at rates significantly higher and beyond the Halveth baseline. The acceleration was documented across six separate survey points over an eighteen-month period, with projections that placed the Durnath pass at serious risk of corruption infiltration within three to five years rather than the two to three decades the Halveth survey suggested. The surveyor's recommendations were explicit: the council must take immediate action. Nonessential travel through the southern zones must be suspended. Review of all active expeditions operating in the affected zones.

Eiran's expedition commission had been signed four months after this report was filed and signed off on. By Valdris.

Seraphine set the report on the table. The reading room remained cold, the stone walls holding the chill of the lower floors regardless of the season. She shivered. The cold burrowed past her skin, into her center. Her shivering turned to shaking as she sat staring at the document.

Valdris had sent Eiran into the southern pass with a risk assessment that was wrong, built on information that was incorrect. Eiran had gone because he trusted the assessment. He'd had no reason not to. The man who had commissioned the expedition looked at him at the reception with that false warmth and told him the council had been following his work with considerable interest.

Eventually, Seraphine's hands stilled. The cold was still there, bone-deep. She'd thought her anger, her grief, would burn.

Seraphine opened her notebook and began to copy the report by hand. She worked slowly, writing down every figure, every survey point, every date, every notation, every signature. She copied the surveyor's recommendations at the end of the report in full, the filing codes, the cross-reference notation that had led her here in the first place. When she finished, she read her copy against the original, line by line, and found it was exact.

She closed her notebook and put it in her satchel's inner pocket, against the lining. Then, she replaced the original document in its exact position in the delivered stack, at the same angle, and with the same slight curl in the bottom right corner. Seraphine gathered her notebooks and her pen. She left the materials she'd requested at the reading table, like she'd been instructed to do, and signed out at the admissions register.

Outside, Seraphine blinked against the brightness of Grauradur's light. The city was fully in its day. The light off the canal shone brightly on every surface. She stood on the polished stone steps and let the light hit her face. Then she put the satchel strap over her shoulder and walked home.

# CHAPTER
# FIFTEEN

Seraphine requested a formal meeting with Valdris the next day. When the secretary asked her about the nature of her request, she told him it was a project update and would only require half an hour of the councilor's time. Valdris's secretary sent a notice later that afternoon, confirming the location and time of her appointment. Third floor meeting chamber in the government quarter, two days from now.

She arrived at five minutes to ten o'clock with the copy of the report in her coat's inner pocket, having ripped the pages out of her notebook.

The meeting chamber was a room designed to conduct serious business without appearing to. The ceilings were vaulted, the windows tall and arched, letting in soft morning light. Furniture in rich, creamy fabrics scattered about the chamber, and a highly polished table made from a light wood in the room's center. Valdris was already there when she entered, his wings extended to their full, resplendent length. They seemed to shimmer in the soft light, their white almost identical to the buildings of polished marble that made up the government quarter.

Seraphine was not impressed.

He stood when she came in and gestured to the chair across from his. He offered her tea from an exquisitely arranged tray, which she declined. He poured himself a cup and the steam swirled above the rim, letting the scent of jasmine float through the room.

Seraphine withdrew the copy of the report, unfolded it, and set it on the table between them. She didn't say anything.

Valdris looked at the document, then at her. Something in her expression must have told him enough, because he didn't bother to read it.

"How did you find it?"

"The primary index," she said. "Survey materials related to active expedition commissions are required to be cross-referenced. This one was not. The absence was more legible than the document would have been if it had been filed correctly." She held his gaze. "You hid it in plain sight, which works until someone knows to look for what is missing rather than what is present."

Something moved across his face. Seraphine recognized it as irritation at being outmaneuvered by the precise method he should have anticipated.

His wings flexed, sending a draft through the room. "I see," he said.

"You reviewed this report four months before Eiran's expedition was initiated."

"Yes."

The room fell into silence. Outside, the government quarter hummed with fae conducting their business.

Seraphine studied Valdris's face. He met her gaze steadily, as if he had nothing to hide.

"The surveyor's recommendations were clear," Seraphine finally said.

The tea in front of Valdris had stopped steaming. He let it sit, untouched, in front of him.

"Eiran's expedition was not reviewed against this data."

Valdris fingered the delicate silver chain that hung down his robes. "No. It was not."

She had expected denial, or placating statements meant to soothe her, or distract her from the report. Threats, even. Seraphine had prepared for all of that. His directness was harder to navigate, which she suspected he understood.

"Why?" she asked quietly.

"The projections were alarming. Three to five years until the pass was seriously compromised? If that information had become public, it would have triggered emergency protocols. There would have to be full public disclosure, and a suspension on all southern travel. In short, there would have been panic."

Seraphine felt the ice harden in her chest.

Valdris continued. "There also would have been an independent audit of every commission and policy decision concerning boundary regions and how the corruption was addressed for the past decade. Including decisions that allowed the corruption to accelerate to this point and why the council did not intervene sooner. Decisions made and not made by those who are still sitting on that council."

"Including you."

"Including me."

Seraphine received his admission with the same numbness she'd felt since first reading the report days ago. "So, you buried it."

"I filed it in location that limited its circulation. I thought the expedition would produce current data that would supersede this report's findings. The situation would be better addressed with Eiran's results in hand than with a suppressed report and a council in crisis."

"Eiran died because he did not have adequate information. Because the risk assessment implied that it was safe for him to go."

Guilt flashed then in Valdris's face. In the lines by his mouth and the ones on the outer corners of his eyes. He grew heavier for a moment, weighed down by his culpability. Then it was gone.

"When Eiran died, the report became something I could not undo. I could only determine what happened next." Valdris looked at the copy between them. "Which is why we commissioned you for help. It's why you're sitting in this room."

"You commissioned me to manage the consequences of the report." She clenched her hands together to keep from shivering. Why was she so cold?

"I commissioned you because the corruption is real and accelerating. Our best hope now is to create something to contain or destroy it. You are now the best available response. Both of those things are true."

"But they are no equivalent," Seraphine said, the ice in her heart creeping into her tone.

"No. They are not." Valdris sat back in his chair. His eyes narrowed slightly, assessing her. Then, having decided that directness was the only currency she was going to deal in, asked, "What are you going to do with it?"

"I haven't decided."

"You came here to tell me you have it, not to negotiate. You already know what you're going to do, and you wanted me to know that you know. So." He leaned forward in his chair once more. "What are you going to do?"

Seraphine picked up the report and returned it to the safety of her pocket. "I am going to honor the commission because it is necessary. As you said, the corruption is real and spreading. Tenebris and Grauradur still needs what you hope to provide." She flexed her fingers. "When the commission is complete and functioning, I will decide what happens with the report."

Valdris nodded. The silver chain at his neck shifted against his robes. "You're a practical one."

"I'm an artificer. Practicality is all I deal in." She stood. "Don't interfere with the commission. Don't delay the materials or send anyone to inspect the work or review the methodology. I will create an object that will address the problem, and you will not impede any part of that process."

"Agreed."

She left him sitting in the good furniture with his cold tea, and walked out into the government quarter's wide, pale streets.

THE AFTERNOON LIGHT WAS LOW. Spring was a few weeks off still. The air still had winter's bite, but the sun felt warm on her face. A promise of warmer days ahead. Seraphine hung her coat on the hook by the door and went to her bench.

Eiran's notebook was where she always left it, next to her tools. She had read the survey notes in their entirety over the past several weeks. His gradient maps, field observations, and the account of the third zone. But she had not read the entire notebook. There were sections she had approached then set aside. Places where the handwriting changed character in a way she recognized and had not been ready for.

She opened the journal to one of those places now.

A deviation from his field notes, tucked between two pages of data as though he had written it in an available space rather than intending for it to be found. There were four paragraphs, and her name was not in them, but she recognized herself in every line.

He had written about the way she worked. The focus she brought to a piece when the work was demanding, the way her hands blurred when she stopped consulting her notes and started listening to the thing inside her. He had written about their discussion about how she worked, about discipline versus feeling. He said had had been right, but that she also had been right. Watching her work had shown him that they were not opposing viewpoints, but sequential positions and that she moved between them without noticing she was doing it, which he found remarkable.

In the last paragraph he wrote: *She thinks precision is its own end. I think precision is what she uses to protect the other thing, the part that actually makes the work extraordinary. Because the other thing is harder to defend and she has learned not to leave it exposed. I don't know if she knows I can see it. I suspect she does and has decided to allow it. That seems right for her.*

Seraphine read it over and over again until the words had branded themselves into her mind. She put the notebook down and sat at the bench. She flipped open her last notebook. The one where she had tables and figures in the front.

All that was missing were her sketches and diagrams for the object that she would make.

The picture of it began to take shape in her mind. The materials, the welding, the specific way it must be made to balance the growing corruption. Something that could anchor the magic that had been lost.

Seraphine picked up her drafting pencils and sketched, her hands flying over the paper.

# SIXTEEN

Seraphine sketched until the oil lamp demanded refilling. She grappled with the notion of anchoring, of taking something lost and giving it a home. What she needed was a way to channel the magic. What object, or system of objects, could take magic in and send it out in every direction simultaneously? Not as a single beam but as a network of fine threads reaching into soil and stone and air with the persistence of something alive rather than the duration of something enchanted.

She'd filled twelve pages with sketches, none of them useful, and was finally forced to abandon the question for the night when her stomach growled. Reluctantly, she went downstairs to find something to eat.

As she cooked a simple meal, vegetable soup where she threw in whatever she had that was still fresh, she combed through her notes and the research she had compiled. Corruption was unanchored magic. It spread because it had no fixed point, no source it was tethered to, and in its untethering, it consumed whatever it could reach. Every approach she had read in the archive texts attacked the symptom rather than the condition. Wards pushed corruption back from specific locations without addressing the underlying imbalance. Containment fields required constant magical maintenance and failed catastrophically when that maintenance lapsed. Purification rituals worked on small, corrupted areas but scaled badly and left the treated area vulnerable to reinfection because the conditions that had allowed corruption to take hold had not changed.

None of it was wrong, exactly. It was all just insufficient.

She sat at her kitchen table and dipped a slice of bread into her bowl. She ate without tasting it.

The corruption needed to be counterbalanced. Something to restore the condition that corruption had disrupted, the anchored light that the land had been severed from. Not a single point of restoration, which would be too fragile and too limited, but something distributed. Threaded through the landscape the way corruption threaded through it, pervasive and persistent and self-sustaining.

She was washing the last dish when it arrived.

Not a mirror in the conventional sense. A mirror reflected. Reflection was passive, a simple return of what was already present, and it accomplished nothing she needed. What she needed was *refraction*. A surface that took light in and bent it, broke it apart and sent it outward at every angle simultaneously, the way a prism broke a single beam into spectrum, the way water broke sunlight into the dappled patterns she had watched on the underside of the canal bridges every morning for fifteen years.

A refractive surface of sufficient scale and magical purity, anchored in Tenebris, could do what nothing in the archive had described. It could distribute anchored light through the landscape continuously, without maintenance, without lapsing, because the distribution would be the object's fundamental function rather than an enchantment layered over a passive material.

She set the dish down and dried her hands. She went upstairs and picked up her pen.

Seraphine worked until three o'clock in the morning, and when she went to bed she lay in the dark and thought about the word *mirror*. It was not quite right, but it was the closest word available. She decided it would do for now.

A WEEK PASSED, then two. Crocuses pushed their way up from muddy earth, their white and purple blooms heralding the arrival of the early days of spring. The light that danced off the canal and into the workshop grew stronger, brighter.

Seraphine finished her sketches and the materials arrived in a timely manner. Her first model of the mirror shattered.

She had constructed it from standard workshop glass set in a copper frame. Small enough to hold in both hands and enchanted with what she was calling the refractive principle in her notes. The magic was simple and the model was a test. She had not expected it to work on the first attempt. However, she had not expected it to fail in the way it did. Structurally, the mirror was fine. There was no power over-load, as she had anticipated, but a sort of rejection. The enchantment and the glass parted from one another clearly, like oil and water.

Seraphine swept the shattered pieces into the waste bin

and documented what had happened. Then, she built another one.

The second model used different glass sourced from the guild's specialist on the east side of the canal, who kept materials that standard commission work typically did not require. The enchantment held for six hours before the structure destabilized. The light inside the glass lost its organization and scattered randomly rather than evenly. Seraphine watched it fail, noting the exact manner of its collapse and the way the light scattered then became chaotic. The relationship between the material's magical tolerance and the enchantment's structural demands needed to be brought into alignment.

Seraphine built three more models. The fifth lasted two days before the frame warped and the glass cracked. She noted these failures, too.

As the models accumulated in her waste bin, her understanding of the problem grew. She knew from years of work that the solution would be found through a series of failures rather than through the arrival of a correct answer. So, she kept trying.

She knew there was something she was missing. Her mind, during the hours between dreaming and waking, returned to two texts she had read during her initial research. One she had noted with casual interest but not put any stock in because it was only cross-reference with one other document about alloy sourcing. It was an early documentation of the artificer's craft, so old the binding had been replaced at least once, and the text itself was a copy, the original long gone. Between a chart of alloy sources and a list of early guild membership requirements, was a casual mention of an offering or exchange principle.

*The greatest works are not constructed but given into being. Dead materials hold dead magic. A living work requires an equivalent exchange, a living gift. Something that was once animate with power and had chosen to surrender it. The object does not simply receive the gift. Rather, it becomes it.*

A work of the scale she was designing could not be built from standard materials if this principle were, indeed, true. Dead materials hold dead magic. It was an odd, and slightly inaccurate way, to describe artificing.

She found a bit of clarification in a second text, older than the first, its margins filled with the annotations of several generations of readers. The author had distinguished between two stages of creation that most artificers conflated into one.

*The gifted materials build the vessel. They give the work its form, its capacity, its endurance. But a vessel without a soul is only a container. The soul of a great work comes from the artificer alone and cannot be sourced elsewhere. It is the irreplaceable thing. The substance of what the maker has loved and lost and carried. This is not taken. It cannot be taken. It must be given, and the giving must be chosen, or the work remains only itself and does not become more than itself.*

Seraphine had read this passage twice, then set this aside, as it was not corroborated with any other materials or texts that she could find. She turned her thoughts away from these ideas and focused on the next model.

Seraphine ran into near disaster with her fifth model. It happened very suddenly. She heard a sound like a knuckle popping, sharp and coming from the lower left quadrant of the frame. She knelt and looked at the source of the noise. A hairline fracture, barely visible, running from the base of the load-bearing ring upward through the frame at a thirty-degree angle. Not where she'd reinforced. Somewhere she hadn't thought to support, a stress point that only became a stress point at the specific frequency she'd pushed the model to this morning.

She held her hand near the fracture without touching it, close enough to feel the resonance moving through the metal and read what she could from it. The enchantment found a crack and had moved to fill it the way water found a gap in mortar. She couldn't quantify the rate without the Thaumic Meridian, which the university hadn't returned to her. It was, perhaps, somewhere in the third corruption zone in a satchel she'd never see again. What she could do was watch the fracture and count the millimeters.

Two per minute, roughly. Perhaps a fraction more.

Seraphine turned to record the fracturing in her working notebook, bending over her workbench. Her attention on her notes is what saved her face and eyes from damage.

The mirror frame exploded, sending shards of metal and glass shrapnel through the workshop like hail. An enchantment Seraphine had placed the first month she had moved in activated. It had never activated before. A magical barrier sprang up, shielding her materials, the forge, and most of her workbench from the debris.

Seraphine felt the shift in the air just as the mirror detonated, dropping her face into her arms and covering her head. The sound was enormous in the narrow workshop, a crack of displaced air followed by the percussion of metal fragments hitting the walls and ceiling and floor in rapid succession, overlapping impacts too fast to count individually, a brief chaotic hail that lasted perhaps three seconds and then stopped.

She stayed down for a moment longer than she needed to, her arms over her head, her face pressed against the workbench. The barrier enchantment hummed at the edge of her awareness, the magic she'd laid into the workshop's infrastructure fifteen years ago and tested once and never needed again. It held with a steadiness that meant the impact had been significant enough to trigger it fully rather than partially. She straightened slowly and looked at the workshop.

The fifth model was gone. Consumed by a high-energy magical failure that consumed its own materials. Nothing remained of the frame and carefully integrated components except a scorch mark on the floor where the model had stood and a fine metallic dust that caught the afternoon light from the window and hung briefly in the air before settling. The barrier had done its job. Her tools were undisturbed on the bench, her reference texts intact on the shelves, her material stocks behind their protective housings untouched. The eastern wall had taken most of the impact. She'd need to replaster it.

Seraphine checked herself methodically, the way she checked a commission for damage, starting with her hands. A small cut on the back of her left wrist where a fragment had caught her before the barrier closed, shallow and already stopping. Her ears were ringing. Otherwise, she was intact.

She looked at the scorch mark for a while. She'd pushed the fifth model to a frequency she hadn't tested the frame against because she'd been confident in the reinforcement, and that confidence had been wrong. What she'd lost was five days of construction and a significant quantity of high-grade materials. The glass composition alone had cost her the better part of a week's income at current guild rates. She'd sourced the highest grade available and fed it into a model that had just distributed itself across her eastern wall.

Seraphine studied the scorch mark. The failure had told her something the previous four hadn't, which was where the frame's actual breaking point lived. Not the stress points she'd reinforced, not the junctions she'd identified as high-risk from the earlier failures. A section she'd considered sound because her calculations said it would be.

She could fix this. She knew exactly how because she'd watched the fracture begin and read its propagation. In the few seconds before the frame failed, she understood what the metal was trying to tell her. The fracture had run at thirty degrees from the base of the load-bearing ring, which meant the stress was distributing unevenly through the lower quadrant in a way her initial geometry hadn't accounted for. She needed to change the geometry, not just reinforce the existing design. The sixth model would be structurally different from the fifth in ways that went beyond adding material to problem points.

She picked up her notebook and wrote down everything she'd observed as the dust continued to settle around her. When she was finished, she read them back, checking for anything she'd missed while her ears were still ringing.

Seraphine set her notebook down and looked at the eastern wall and at the window. She had perhaps two hours of working daylight left. Not enough to begin the sixth frame tonight. Enough to clean up, and source the materials she'd need and prepare the components for an early start tomorrow.

She made quick work of the dust with an elimination enchantment that collected, strained, and siphoned the now useless material into a container for disposal. The protective barrier had saved her from a potential day's worth of clean up. Seraphine eyed the damaged wall and decided she'd deal with replastering it tomorrow. Then she put on her coat and left for the guild supplier on the east canal. She had more work to do.

A FEW WEEKS later she sat at her bench with the sixth attempt, which had survived far longer than any others but was now showing the same signs of stress that she'd seen in the last model. Seraphine bit her lip and took notes on the stress pattern in the frame and glass. She said aloud, without planning to, "The problem is the frame is doing two jobs and is only built for one."

She knew there was no one in the chair by the window. It remained empty. The book still sat on the windowsill, now curved with the passage of time. She hadn't moved it.

Seraphine didn't understand why she'd spoken her thought aloud, as if he could hear her. But he had offered commentary on all her work, and this was an object she was making with him in mind. He had argued with her, forced her to defend her reasoning and offered insight of his own.

She looked at the model on the bench, then the chair, then back at the mirror. "The frame is load-bearing and energetically active at the same time," she said, knowing that there was no logical reason for her to, but found herself doing it anyway. She felt the emptiness behind her, the distinct lack of presence.

"I need to separate those functions. Two components rather than one. You'd say I should have seen that three models ago."

Only silence met her speech.

"You'd be right," she continued. "I was being stubborn. The single-frame design is more elegant. Simpler. I was prioritizing ease over function, which you would find absurd, I think."

Seraphine picked up her draft pencil and drew the separation in her notebook, dividing the frame into two component functions. "The principle is sound. I've tested it enough times to know."

She knew exactly how he'd respond. He never offered reassurance for its own sake, but he would ask a question. One that pressed at things she hadn't quite said.

*What changed? What does the sixth model tell you that the others have not?*

"It's failing more slowly," she said. "The stress is taking longer to accumulate, which means the enchantment and the material are closer to compatible than they were. I'm on the right path."

Seraphine turned the page in her notebook and started a new diagram. "The material is the remaining problem. Not the enchantment structure or the refractive principle. The frame design will be better once I've separated the functions. The glass isn't right. Glass isn't what this wants to be made of."

She worked until a silver sickle moon rose and stars glimmered in the blue-black sky. She spoke aloud when she needed talking through something and was silent when the work required silence.

THREE DAYS LATER, Seraphine pinned the final drawings to the wall above the bench as twilight settled over the workshop. Seven sheets covered in notations, diagrams, and schematics. She stood back and looked at them as a gentle breeze blew in from the open window.

The object was not a mirror in the conventional sense. It was a refractive surface of significant scale, as tall as she was, built on a separated load-bearing and energy-channeling frame designed to accept magic of large quantities and distribute it outwards in all directions simultaneously. Downward into root, soil, and stone. Upward into air and atmosphere. Across landscape and in threads fine and persistent enough to function as a permanent counterforce to unanchored magic across a wide region. The enchantment structure was the most complex she had ever designed. The material was the last piece of the puzzle. Glass was insufficient.

Seraphine studied the drawings for a long time.

She had made exceptional things before. Eiran had called them extraordinary. The Aldenmere lenses. The Meridian she had built for Eiran, the active pulse design going further than what the commission technically required. She had made things that worked better than they needed to and that she was privately proud of. But this was different.

This was the most significant thing she had ever attempted, and she knew it with the certainty she'd felt when the idea of the refractive principle had first arrived. Her body registered the truth before her mind had finished the calculations. It would either work completely or fail. There was no middle ground. Not with this.

Seraphine looked at the drawings, feeling the emptiness of the chair by the window.

Eiran had noted the difference in her craft when she was thinking logically through a problem versus when she was listening to what the object required.

She squeezed her eyes shut. An unfamiliar wave of frustration rushed through her, as she had been trying for hours to sever filament with blunted wire cutters. She did not know how to access that part of herself on command. But she had a feeling that the work would go much more smoothly if she could.

With a heavy sigh, she opens her eyes, closed the window to the workshop and took the oil lamp downstairs with her. Seraphine turned her attention to the remaining problem she could solve.

She thought of the exchange principle. The one casually mentioned, not cross-reference or corroborated.

*Dead materials hold dead magic.*

Seraphine knew with certainty, based on her failed models. Glass would not do for this mirror.

She would need to make inquiries.

CHAPTER

# SEVENTEEN

Ossin Vaer lived at the edge of Caeledrath's oldest district. Here, the city thinned out as the canal widened into the northern reservoir. The buildings transitioned from the pale, polished order of the government quarter to houses hewn from stone. They had been carved from the mountains themselves, with walls thickened by generations of repair, their stone so weathered they took on the shale color of the ground they stood on.

His house was at the end of a narrow lane. The pale morning light only reached the middle of the lane for half an hour each day. The air was cool and damp. Seraphine found the address in the artificer guild's historical records, which maintained a registry of those who practiced near-extinct magical traditions. His entry was the last in a list of names that dated back four centuries.

Ossin Vaer was currently retired, noted by a small notation on the register. This was the guild's diplomatic term for someone who no longer practiced because there was nothing left of the tradition to practice in.

But Seraphine was not deterred, because Ossin was the last artificer who worked with light, and the mirror demanded a thorough understanding of this principle if she was going to find a material that would conduct light in the way the commission required.

She knocked, but the house remained still. She waited patiently. The seconds ticked on, and just as Seraphine began to wonder if he was out when the door opened.

He was very old. Not in the way of a fae who had lived long and kept most of their earlier appearance, permanently touched by a youthfulness that was inherent in their blood, but in the way of someone who had simply stopped maintaining the effort of looking that way. Age showed in the deep lines of his face and hands, the tarnish of his gray hair, the stoop in his shoulders. His eyes, however, were clear.

"Seraphine," he said, his voice was as harsh as a rockslide. "I've been expecting you."

She had not told him she was coming.

He stood aside and gestured for her to enter.

The house smelled of cedar, old paper, and a cindery quality that she recognized. It was the same smell her workshop carried after she'd finished working on a commission, the smell of magic and enchantment, the residue it left behind. The front room was small and precisely kept. For someone who had lived so long, there were few possessions in Ossin's home. As though he had whittled them down and kept only what had earned its place. Books on two shelves, each one worn with repeated reading. A chair in the corner, a small stool, a low wooden table with an oil lamp. A small potted plant in the window.

Ossin moved to the chair, and Seraphine took the small stool across from him.

She studied him for a moment and relaxed as she realized they were not going to bother with the preliminary stages of a conversation.

Good.

"You know why I'm here," she said. That much had been obvious in the way he'd greeted her at the door.

Ossin placed his spotted hands on his knees. "I know what you're building. Tell me what you know about the offering principle."

Seraphine told him about the passage she had found. She did so perfunctorily, without judgement. But she could not help but add, "There was no other mention of the principle anywhere. As a result, I haven't given it much consideration."

Ossin settled back into his chair. "I see. I advise you to give it almost all your consideration. For the object to work, there must be an offering. It is an old element of our work. It wasn't always called the offering principle. Long before then, it was simply exchange. That is the oldest truth about creation. The finest things are never made without cost. What you give to the object, what you offer it in exchange for its function, is just as important as the materials you use to construct it."

Seraphine looked out at the narrow lane where the light was doing it's one hour of work on the cobblestones, heating them briefly before they'd turn cool once more as the light left them.

"I see," she said finally. "And what of your work?"

"Light weaving began in Caeledrath five hundred years ago. There were perhaps thirty practitioners at its height. By my parent's generation there were eight. By mine, three. The other two are long gone. The practice requires a specific sensitivity that is either present or not. It cannot be taught to someone who doesn't carry it. My children did not have the skills, and neither did theirs." He said this without apparent grief, as if this had been fact long enough to be fully absorbed. "I made my last piece a hundred years ago."

She had read about it. It was, primarily, why she had come. A length of woven light, strong enough to be used in artifice as a material that could bind and shape magic itself. It had been forged, then placed in a cedar box. It was precious.

"You made a length of woven light. Magic made physically coherent and tangible, like strong thread. Capable of being worked into larger structures without losing its own essential properties," Seraphine said.

"Yes." Ossin folded his hands in his lap. "And do you know what happens to a length of woven light that sits in a cedar box under a bed for a hundred years?"

"It waits."

The old fae's eyes sparkled, as if the memory of that light, the appearance of Seraphine, had rekindled a hope long held.

"It does indeed," he said. "I made it knowing it was meant to be a part of something larger than itself. I have waited this long to find out." He stood slowly, and Seraphine rose to help him.

He accepted her arm without comment, as he had learned to accept help without making it into something.

"Come with me," he said. The walked to the bedroom.

Ossin pointed at the bed, and Seraphine bent to retrieve the cedar box. The wood was warm in her hands, yet there was a stillness inside the box, as if the magic it contained had been waiting for so long it had gone very still. It was the stillness of undisturbed, deep water.

"Open it," Ossin said.

Seraphine set the box on the bed. The hinges made no sound as she lifted the lid, letting the scent of cedar swell throughout the room. Inside, folded carefully, was a length of something that was not quite fabric and not quite light, but something in between the two. It was the color of palest dawn and radiated gentle warmth.

She did not touch it. Seraphine looked at the woven light for a long time before she gently closed the box and latched the lid.

"You're certain?"

"I made it to be given," Ossin replied. "I understood that when I made it."

Seraphine held the box. It vibrated slightly, like a purring cat who stretched itself awake after a long nap. It was comforting. "Thank you."

"Before you go..." Ossin peered at her, assessing. "Does it hurt? The work."

Seraphine thought about the model, their shattering, the failures. The talking aloud to herself, to an empty chair. The book she hadn't moved from the windowsill, or the cup she sometimes still reached for when she made tea. "Yes," she said.

Ossin nodded once. "Good. The ones that don't hurt aren't worth making. You begin to understand the law of exchange, then."

Yes. She supposed she was beginning to understand, even if it was not consciously done.

She thanked Ossin once more, put the box carefully into her satchel, and set off for her next destination.

# EIGHTEEN

Seraphine made her way to the south side of the city equipped with an address to find Thessaly Morn next. She lived in a terraced house on a cobbled street that ran parallel to a secondary canal. The district had been the center of the city's textile trade, the most well-known in all of Grauradur. Though the demand for textiles had dwindled, the clack of spindles and looms still echoed throughout the quarter. Buildings here high large ground floors with high ceilings to hold the looms, loading doors and ramps made carrying spools of thread into the workshops easier.

Thessaly was not, primarily, a weaver, but a glass singer. Seraphine had found her through a different route than she'd found Ossin. The guild registers did not have any entries on glass singing, as it was never formally recognized as a guild tradition. But she had found the name family name Morn in a footnote in one of the archive's genealogy records of artificers with passing reference to their ability to sing the glass. Morn's work in the third century of the current council had been considered significant enough to document, but obscure enough that almost no one had. What was detailed about the glass singer's ability matched what Seraphine was looking for, though. The city's residential registry, maintained by the civic records office in the same building as the archive, gave an address.

Seraphine knocked on Thessaly's door as the sun began to leave its peak in a brilliant robin's-egg-blue sky. The woman who answered the door was thin and petite, precise in her movements. Her chestnut hair was clipped short and fell over her pointed ears.

"Can I help you?" she asked, her voice light and airy.

"My name is Seraphine Caell. I am an artificer. I've been given a commission by the council and need to ask you about the disc you made."

Thessaly squinted at her for a moment. Her eyes lingered over the satchel on her shoulder, and Seraphine wondered if she could sense the cedar box inside. Then, having seen something that assured her, Thessaly stepped aside and Seraphine entered the workroom.

It was different from her own workshop. There was no forge, no tools, no jarred materials labelled carefully and stored on shelves. Instead, there was a long, broad table and spools of thread in dozens of colors set on multiple thread racks. Dyes in all shades in clear bottles, and a few large vats for dying fabric lined the western wall.

Lengths of cloth in various stages of completion covered the table in the center of the room, the careful disorder hinting at the active textile work in progress.

Thessaly did not offer her tea. She went to her worktable, moved two bolts of cloth aside, and sat down. She gestured to the seat across from her, and Seraphine was reminded of another time, months ago, where she had done the same for Eiran.

She swallowed against the knot in her throat and took her seat.

"So. What do you want to know?"

Thessaly did not ask about her commission, or how she knew about the object she had made.

"Tell me about the making of your disc."

Thessaly smoothed the edge of a piece of fabric. "I made it sixty-three years ago. My daughter was eight. Her name was Fen." She said the name without softening it, the way you said a name you had learned to carefully carry without flinching. "She had been ill for two years by then. No healer had any answers. We knew, by that point, what the illness would do."

The woman dropped the corner of the mustard yellow fabric she'd been touching and met Seraphine's eyes. "I made it in the month before she died. This," she gestured to the workshop around her, "is my second occupation. Before I worked with textiles, I was a glass singer. I made beautiful things with the glass. Melting it, shaping it. Items of beauty that folk would pay a pretty dinar for. I was at the height of my ability when it happened."

"I wanted to make Fen something pretty to look at. She was fading quickly, and she liked little trinkets and baubles. So, I sang over the little piece of glass, not really knowing what I would make her. But I sang over it for three days. Every note I had."

Seraphine held silent, noting the weight of the woman's grief. It was long worn, but that did not make it any less heavy.

"Glass singing was special. I made things of specific

magical resonance. Singing restructures the material, aligning the glass with the singer's intention during its making. That intention determines what the glass remembers."

Thessaly blinked, her blue eyes growing distant with memory. "I sang in the room where Fen was sleeping. It was summer. She woke up while I was working and watched me finish. She asked me what I was making, and I told her I was making something to give her light and comfort. She said that sounded right."

Her hands stilled on the table. Her throat bobbed, then she continued. "She died a few days later. She had her father's eyes, and she could name every bird that came to the garden window just by the song they sang. She said it sounded right. I have no doubt she would have been a fine glass singer, had she lived."

The workroom was quiet, save for the trill of birdsong.

"I stopped singing after that. I had nothing left to sing with. The voice is still there, in a technical sense, but the thing that made it glass singing, instead of simply singing, is gone." Thessaly stated this without self-pity. It was simply a result of what the grief had done to her.

"I'm sorry," Seraphine said, because she was.

"Yes. Those of us who have lost someone, you can tell. I'm sorry for yours as well."

Seraphine had not come to talk about their shared grief. "Thank you," she said. She didn't want to be impolite.

The two women sat in the workroom. Dust motes swirled in the air between them.

"Where is the disc?" Seraphine finally asked.

Thessaly rose wordlessly and walked to a cabinet against the far wall, made of plain wood and used for practical storage rather than display. She opened the lower door and reached in without looking, withdrawing an object wrapped in undyed cloth. She set it on the table between them.

Seraphine did not unwrap it immediately. She set her hand on the wrappings and felt the warmth it emanated. It was persistent, having sung at a frequency too low to hear for the past six decades. Her gaze drifted the Thessaly.

"It's been warm since I've made it. Fen was sleeping, and my intentions—well. This was the result."

Neither of them said what they were both thinking about, which was the weight of objects that had been made in the presence of someone who was gone. What it meant to hold them. And to let them go.

Thessaly looked at the cloth-wrapped disc of glass, then expectantly at Seraphine.

Seraphine knew the gravity of what she had to ask, but it was necessary. She swallowed, then asked, "May I use your sung glass in the mirror I am making?"

"A mirror?"

"Yes. It's what I am calling it, as it's the closest thing to what I am making. An object to rebalance the corruption in Tenebris that is spreading towards Grauradur." Seraphine was unsure if she should be telling Thessaly about the particulars of the commission, but the woman across from her deserved to know, if she was to give her the object she'd made for her dying daughter.

Thessaly was quiet for a moment. "A mirror." She nodded once, her mind made up. "Fen would have liked to know it was going toward the light. She would have thought that was exactly right." She pushed the cloth wrappings toward Seraphine. "Take it. I have been waiting to say that to someone for a very long time."

Seraphine picked up the sung disc. The warmth came through the cloth steadily. She placed it gently in her satchel. "Thank you." It was insufficient, but it was all there was.

Thessaly stood and went back to attending the cloth bolts at her worktable, taking up her shears. Seraphine understood the visit was complete and saw herself out.

She walked home as the sun set, turning the streets of Caeledrath distinctly fae. It was during the hours of sunset that the city truly looked gods-touched, living up to its name. Pale stone buildings, polished and gleaming glowed like jewels mined from a cave.

Seraphine felt the warmth of the disc even through her satchel as it rested against her hip. Seraphine took the long route home, along the main canal, because she wasn't quite ready to be back in the workshop. The sunset on the canal sparkled, closer to gold than silver, and Seraphine found she wanted to think and walk at the same time. She always found difficult thoughts best solved with movement.

She thought about Fen, who had been eight years old, bore her father's eyes, and had an affinity for birdsong. She thought about Thessaly, and what it meant to make something in the presence of happiness. The disc was warm because Fen had been there when it was made. Thessaly had been singing at the height of her ability, in a summer room with her daughter watching, and that specific set of factors, unreplaceable and unique, had produced what Seraphine now kept in her satchel. The combination of love, skill, and the terrible, bittersweet knowledge of what was coming had gone into the glass and stayed there for sixty-three years. Quietly humming with what had been poured into it.

Seraphine studied her own hand as she turned off the

main canal street. They had made things in the presence of happiness, and in the grief that she'd been left with.

The market stalls were closing, the last little boats were tied up to their moorings. Children called to one another as they ran back home for dinner. The city continued to hum with life as Seraphine made it to her own door. She walked up the stairs, her footsteps echoing with familiar creaks, the disc warm against her hip.

CHAPTER

# NINETEEN

Seraphine spent three days after Thessaly's with the cedar box and the glass disc on her bench, the mirror's schematic pinned to the wall, and the growing certainty that something was still missing.

She had a length of woven light, which would provide the mirror's distribution structure. The sung disc would provide the refractive surface's core resonance. Both materials were extraordinary, and both had been gifted willingly to her. They satisfied the offering principle that Ossin had demanded she take into better account. On paper, the design was complete. She should have been ready to begin.

Seraphine stood at the bench on the third morning with her notes in front of her, the two materials beside them, and studied her drawings. Something in her body, which she had gradually learned to trust over the past decades of her work, told her that it was not yet right. As it was, the mirror would not hold.

She sat down and worked through it again methodically. She looked at the dual frame, the glass, the lines of enchant-

140

ment, her conversion tables, the calibration measurements. The light-weaving would integrate into the frame structure and provide the distribution network. The glass disc would form the refractive core and maintain the mirror's primary function of refraction at a steady rate that she had calculated over the course of a day of examining Thessaly's work. Together, they would produce the power and precision necessary.

But something was still *missing*.

Seraphine stood in front of the designs and looked at the anchoring structure, tapping it with her finger.

There it was.

The distribution network needed an origin point, a frequency from which the light could spread outward into Tenebris. The mirror would be placed there, a land that had been severed from its light source at a specific time. The corruption that had filled the resulting absence had been there long enough to become the landscape's dominant magic condition. A mirror projecting the wrong frequency would be pushing light against a resistant medium. One that was well-established and had become the new accepted state of being. The landscape would not recognize the mirror's distribution and would push back.

She needed the mirror to project a frequency that the land already knew. A frequency from before the severing, before the corruption spread. Before the landscape had lost the thing it was supposed to be connected to.

Seraphine sat back down and checked her notes. She half-remembered something from the archives. Something in a geological survey text about pre-council Grauradur, a brief mention of stone formations in the oldest parts of Caeledrath that predated the geographical separation of

Grauradur and Tenebris by the mountains. Stone that was formed when the two lands had been one continuous landscape, carrying the magical resonance between them.

There. A reference code pulled from a footnote. She grabbed her notebooks and her satchel and left for the archives.

THE GEOLOGICAL SURVEY holdings took an additional two days to work through properly. What Seraphine found confirmed what the footnote suggested and added a detail that changed the material question from theoretical to urgent. Pre-separation stone still existed in Caeledrath in its architectural foundations, in the oldest buildings in the city, but those were inaccessible and could not be removed without compromising the buildings themselves. The only stone she could identify that would work was a portable fragment, documented in a single field report from forty years ago. An expedition crossing of the southern pass that had collected geographical samples from scree fields at the mouth of the pass.

The author of the report was a magical ecologist named Peran Meras. Seraphine looked him up in the faculty register and found that he was retired. However, he still resided in the faculty quarter, as he was a professor emeritus.

She read the entire report, noting that Professor Meras understood that the geological context mattered as much as the sample itself. The fragment of stone she needed was item seven, a grey stone approximately four centimeters wide, seven centimeters long. It had anomalous magical resonance that was inconsistent with Grauradur's current geological foundations, which meant the stone must come from the land in Tenebris.

There was an additional note that the fragment was retained by the expedition leader for further study.

Meras had the stone still in his possession and had kept it for forty years.

Seraphine frowned. Something like this should be kept in the archeological archives. Yet, Meras had kept it.

She was left with concern. She had one chance. She had the woven light, the glass, and she was not going to find a second stone fragment. Not in the time available, and possibly not at all. The mirror's anchoring structure required these specific materials.

The mirror's anchoring structure required pre-separation stone, and the only one she could acquire belonged to a retired professor who had carried it home from Tenebris four decades ago.

Seraphine tidied her workstation, packed her notes, and left to find him.

She did not look across the courtyard at Eiran's office when she passed. Her eyes slid across small ceramic tiles imprinted with names as she walked down the hall.

She found Meras on the third floor, last door on the left. She knocked. There was a moment's pause. Then, "It's open."

He sat at a desk by the window. His face bore some lines of age, making him look more rugged than those fae who were government officials, who had only known the comfort of their offices and had not gone on perilous expeditions to the southern borders. Meras kept his hair long on top, pulled back into a bun. He wore a knit sweater with a fraying left pocket that reminded her of a green coat.

Meras looked over his reading glasses. "You're the artificer."

"I am Seraphine Caell."

"Sit down, then."

The desk was covered in the organized disorder of active research. Books flagged with color-coded paper slips, an open notebook, and several survey maps weighted at the corners with field stones.

Seraphine spied the stone she was here for immediately, four centimeters by seven centimeters, a deeper gray than the others, laying on the top right corner of a map. She felt the warmth from across the desk. The same that had emanated from the cedar box and the glass disc.

"You want the stone," he said.

Seraphine did not bother questioning how he knew this. People talked, and by now it was no secret that she was an artificer commissioned by the council and had visited several specialists in the past week. What he thought about her or her visit was inconsequential. She was indeed here for the stone.

"I want to talk to you about it first," she said.

"Talking about it and giving it to you are two different things." Professor Meras took his glasses off. "What do you know about it?"

Seraphine told him about the mirror's anchoring structure, the pre-separation resonance, and why the specific frequency was necessary. She was precise and complete in her explanations. He was a well-experienced scholar who worked with geological materials, and he would know if she approximated. And because she had one attempt at this conversation, she was not going to was it on approximation.

He listened without interrupting. When she finished, he

asked, "The distribution mechanism depends on the anchor having a resonance that the land recognizes?"

"Yes," she said. "The stone carries the frequency of the magic Tenebris was connected to before it was severed from it. The mirror needs that specific frequency to distribute magic into the landscape rather than against it."

"Like a key."

"Yes."

Meras looked at the stone. "My wife found it on the return crossing. I was in poor condition. The corruption had gotten into the lower pass further than we'd mapped out. I'd taken a bad exposure crossing back through it. Do you know what the corruption does, Ms. Caell?"

Seraphine's chest tightened. Meras was simply posing the question as a professor might ask his student, but she had not dwelt on what it might have been like for Eiran. She had not wanted to picture it. But she had, during her research, read the surveys and the accounts.

"Mist. So thick you cannot see more than a few centimeters in front of you. And toxic. Most described it as acid eating away at their lungs."

Meras's eyes grew distant. He nodded. "Not only that, but it disorients. The fog enters the brain, limiting its function. It clouds judgement, senses, memory. My wife was waiting at the northern mouth with the support team, and she found the stone in the scree field while they were making camp." He brushed a finger over the spot on the map. "She said it was warm. She put in my hand when I was barely conscious. She said I improved greatly after that. Much faster than the physician we'd brought along expected. She believed the stone was the reason."

"What do you believe?"

"I believe Tessa was more preceptive than most fae I'd encountered, and her instincts about magical objects were better than mine." He brought his gaze to Seraphine's, his eyes sharp once more. "I believe she was probably right. I also believe I have spent the last forty years uncertain whether I was worth saving, which is a separate question from whether the stone saved me."

From below came the muffled sounds of people going about their evening routines, doors closing, footsteps on the stairs, muted conversations.

"You don't have to give it to me," Seraphine said.

"I'm aware." He picked up a cup of cold tea, squinted at it, then set it down. "Without it, what will your mirror do?"

"The mirror projects magical frequency, visible as light. The corruption will push back against the projected light and eventually win. Distributed light threaded into the landscape at the right frequency is self-sustaining. The corruption can't displace something already inside the structure of the place."

Professor Meras picked up the stone and turned it over in his hand, once. A gesture that he had likely performed a hundred times in the last forty years. "Tessa believed in useful things. She had no patience for objects kept for sentiment when they could be doing something." He set the stone down on the desk between them. "But she kept this. She thought the stone was doing something. Keeping me well. Keeping me here."

Pain flashed across his face. "She's been gone twelve years and it's the last object I have that she touched with intention. That is not a good enough reason to withhold it from something that needs it."

"It is a reason," Seraphine said. "It doesn't have to be good enough or not good enough. It's simply true."

Meras's eyes narrowed, reassessing the conversation and the person across from him. "You're not going to tell me the greater good outweighs personal attachment?"

"No."

The huff of a humorless laugh escaped him. "Most fae would."

"Most fae would be arguing a position. I'm not here to argue you into anything." Seraphine looked at the stone. "I need it. I've told you why. What you do with that is yours."

Meras put his glasses back on and looked at his survey maps for a moment. Forty years of work in careful notation, in the writing of someone who had gone into Tenebris, come back, and spent the rest of his life trying to understand what he had seen there.

"The mirror. If it works, what happens to Tenebris?"

"The corruption recedes. Not immediately or completely. The light is distributed into the landscape, the balance shifts over time, and the corruption loses ground rather than gaining it. The fae living there get more time, and more of the land back."

Meras picked up the stone once more and ran his thumb across the surface. It was a gesture that was old, habitual. He held it out between them. "If it works, I want to know."

Seraphine held out her hand. It was warm as Meras placed it in her palm.

"I shall."

The professor turned back to his survey maps.

Seraphine thanked him and saw herself out. She walked home with the stone in her pocket and her hand around it, the warmth steady against her palm all the way along the canal path, up the stairs, and into the workshop.

CHAPTER

# TWENTY

Seraphine began constructing the mirror on the summer solstice, the day of long light. She needed to work by it as many hours as the day would give her. The windows were open, and the canal sent beaming rays of sunlight through the workshop in the way it did in summer. Luminous in a way that cold winter sunlight was not.

She cleared her central workstation entirely. The mirror's frame components laid out in order of assembly. Each piece labeled in her handwriting, the materials separated and wrapped, placed in the sequence she would need them. At the far end of the bench, the cedar box sat open, the length of woven light glowing inside. The glass disc sat beside it on its cloth wrapping, and the stone sat beside that. Eiran's notebook lay on the far end where it always was, and where it would say for the duration of the construction.

The forge was burning hot, and Seraphine activated the air flow and exchange system that would carry the hot fumes outside and leave the workshop cool enough to be in.

Everything was ready. Seraphine picked up the first component and began.

She set to work first on the load-bearing frame, then the thermal regulation housing, the two functions separated as she had designed them. Each component precisely fitted before she moved to the next. The construction required sustained attention but left her mind free enough to contemplate other things. She always thought best with her hands occupied. She replayed her interactions with Ossin, Thessaly, and Meras, thinking about what they had given

Seraphine was fitting the third joint of the load-bearing frame, holding it steady while the binding set, when she thought of him without warning. A specific image surfaced, one that was mundane but comforting in its ordinariness. Eiran at the kitchen table with a survey map spread across it and his elbow planted in the butter dish, which he did not notice. His concentration, the way it made him blind to everything adjacent to the thing he was thinking about.

She had been irritated about the butter dish.

She held the joint steady. The binding set. She moved to the next one.

By late afternoon, the frame was complete. She stood back and scrutinized it. The load-bearing structure was good. Clean, and precisely curved, all joints hidden by carefully designed interlocking components that made it look like the frame was made of a single oval of shining silver. The thermal housing regulation fitting flush within it, like an interior ring.

The two systems were separate and properly portioned.

What's more, the frame looked beautiful. Scrolls and intricate designs she had not intended had emerged as she worked. The metal bent almost on its own, wanting to fall into the shape of ornate flourishes. Seraphine had fought the instinct for only a moment. Then she stopped fighting it because she did not want the mirror to simply exist. She wanted it to be exceptional.

Seraphine ate something standing at the kitchen bench downstairs without tasting it, then went back up and began the light-weaving integration. She wanted to complete it before the sun set, because using the length of woven light required her to see what she was doing and a lamp, though adequate, was not what she preferred for the most delicate work.

Ossin Vaer's light-weaving was more responsive than she had expected. It settled into the frame's distribution channels, cleverly hidden on the interlocking frames and in the scrollwork and flourishes. Her job was less to place it than to guide it, but she had to be very precise.

But she thought about Eiran's hands reorganizing her supply shelf. The way he tested the weight of each jar before he moved it, keeping the lids level. She had moved the copper filings back afterward, which she had known even at the time was not about him fiddling with her system.

The light-weaving settled into the first distribution channel. She moved to the second.

She worked until the lamp needed filling, and then past it, by feel as much as by sight, until the integration was complete and the frame stood finished, leaning up against the bench, as tall as she was. The light was threaded through it in patterns too fine to see, but visible in aggregate as a faint luminosity that had not been there before. The frame shone with an inner light.

Seraphine fell into bed without eating and slept immediately. She did not dream.

THE NEXT DAY, she began before the sun had fully risen. Tying her hair back into its braid, she looked at the glass disc. Today, she would integrate it into the mirror's refractive surface. It was the most intricate task of the entire project. Seraphine had been thinking about the sequence since she'd sat in Thessaly's workshop and felt the disc emanating its warmth through the cloth. She knew the approach she was going to take and had known it for days. But knowing did not make the execution less demanding.

Seraphine moved to the forge and began melting the powders and minerals she would use for the reflective surface. The materials liquified and she prepared the mold. The sung disc required her to match its frequency before she could work with it. Thessaly Morn had sung it at a specific pitch sixty-three years ago, and the glass remembered. Seraphine had to find that pitch with her own magic before the disc would accept her handling.

It took her a few tries. She had rarely communicated with her magic this way, consciously accessing it and asking it to do something for her. Usually, the magic flowed through her, when she entered a state of creation that did not require her to consult her notes.

When she did find the correct frequency, the memory arrived without warning. Eiran's office, the desk cleared except for the filter she had for him, placed to one side where it was not in the way but was visible. She had stood in the middle of his office for a full minute looking at that placement before she picked up the paper she had come to return and left without touching anything else.

The disc's frequency locked with hers. The metal began to move, integrating into the rest of the mirror's materials. She readied a bottle of spray solvent, ready to coat the melted glass as it hardened. Seraphine checked the temperature of the glass, holding the right frequency, and the memory of Eiran's office at the forefront of her mind. The glass hardened.

She sprayed the surface and began to polish it, letting it hum as she passed her cloth over it. The glass melded with the sides of the frame, integrating in the same way the length of woven light had yesterday. Seamlessly, and without much effort on her part.

"I'm glad I gave it to you," she whispered, not conscious that she was speaking aloud. "I'm glad it was on your desk."

Seraphine set down her cloth. The mirror hummed. It was not loud, but it was there. A soft vibration that echoed through the workshop and her ribs.

She had not realized the mirror would hum, but there were some things one could not account for. She checked the frame and the resonance of the glass. They were perfect.

All she had left was the stone. This step required stillness more than skill. She needed sustained, careful attention to hold the stone in position while the anchoring structure recognized the pre-separation frequency of the stone and drew it in.

She picked up the stone and set it into the anchoring housing, the space she'd calibrated against the frequency recorded in Peran Meras's field report. She set the frame's enchantment to the pre-separation resonance he'd specified. This was the key the mirror needed to distribute light into Tenebris rather than push against it. She held the stone in position, called the enchantment forward, and waited for the integration to begin.

The mirror hummed around her. The frame's light-weaving pulsed in its distribution channels, the disc, integrated into the glass, held Thessaly Morn's frequency steady, everything operating exactly as she'd designed it.

The stone did nothing.

She held it longer, adjusting the angle of contact by fractions, running the integration enchantment again from the first step. The housing geometry was precise. The frequency she'd calibrated into the metal matched the archive reading. She checked the stone's current resonance, using a hastily completed version of the Thaumic Meridian, and found it consistent with what she'd built the structure to receive. Everything was correct, by every measure she had, but the stone and the mirror simply declined to connect.

She sat down on the floor with her back against the workbench and stayed there for a while with the stone in her hands. It should work, and she couldn't explain why. She reached up a hand for her notes and poured over them, looking for what she might have missed.

When that failed, she returned to the archive.

Seraphine checked her notes against Meras's field report. The frequency reading was right. She'd built the anchoring structure around that reading to four decimal places. She read his notation again slowly, not looking for the number this time but for the conditions of measurement. He'd taken the reading in the scree field at the mouth of the Durnath, after he'd recovered enough from his brush with the corruption. The instruments he'd used was documented in his equipment list: a standard resonance probe, the kind every field scholar carried forty years ago, with a calibration tolerance of roughly half a percent across the full spectrum.

She took out her hastily made copy of the Thaumic Meridian and held it over the page. The ambient resonance that documents absorbed from their contents over decades of proximity was something most artificers never thought to measure. Seraphine measured it now because she'd run out of other variables. The dials spun, hitting on the change in frequency and the reading came back in seconds. The frequency the paper had absorbed from years of proximity to its own data matched what she'd calibrated against.

The reading the stone currently carried did not.

The difference was under three percent across the full spectrum, small enough that a standard probe wouldn't catch it, small enough that it hadn't registered on her initial checks because she'd been looking for significant discrepancies rather than fine ones. She worked through what the difference meant, tracking it across frequencies the way she'd track a crack through a weld.

The stone's pre-separation resonance was intact. That hadn't changed. What had changed was everything layered around it, frequencies that had accrued over decades the way minerals accreted around a crystal's core, altering the outer structure while leaving the original unchanged. She'd built the anchoring housing to receive the core, and the accreted layers had nowhere to seat themselves, which meant the stone couldn't fully integrate. The mirror didn't recognize it as the key it was.

Seraphine concluded that forty years in Peran Meras's rooms had done this. His hands, his grief, his habit of carrying the object because his wife had believed it would keep him alive. The stone hadn't simply been stored for all those years. It had been held, which was a different thing entirely, and holding left traces that a standard instrument wouldn't catch and that Meras himself would never have had instruments precise enough to notice.

She'd calibrated the mirror's housing against the available documentation, but she needed to calibrate it against what the stone actually was, right now, in her workshop. She gathered her notes and left the archive.

SERAPHINE DISMANTLED the anchoring structure that night, working carefully because a completed structure resisted being reopened and rushing would damage what she was trying to fix. She stripped the enchantments out of the metal pass by pass, twelve hours of work undone over four, keeping the geometric housing intact and removing only the enchantment layered into the metal. The mirror held steady around the gap, the light-weaving and the disc continuing their work, indifferent to what she was doing at the base.

The stone sat on the corner of the bench while she worked, warm enough that she could feel it when she passed close. She rebuilt the housing to receive the stone as it currently was pre-separation resonance at the core, forty years handling and energy layered around it. Tessa's belief and Meras's survival and the grief of a man who'd spent four decades uncertain he deserved to keep living. All of it woven into the frequencies she was now encoding into metal.

On the morning of the third day of rebuilding, she set the stone into the housing and held it there.

The integration began immediately, the frequencies aligning with a cleanness she felt through her palms before she registered it consciously. The pre-separation resonance seated first, then the outer layers found their positions in sequence, each one drawing in as the housing recognized it.

There was nothing for her hands to do but hold the stone as the enchantment did its work, and nothing for her mind to do but wait. Her mind, given nothing to do, went immediately to the last morning and the sound of the street door closing.

She had been looking at her notes when she heard it. She hadn't even looked up from them, and then the door was closed and he was gone. There would be time for the other things when he returned, she'd thought.

She held the stone steady, and the anchoring structure drew the frequency in.

Outside, the canal moved slowly in the heat. The air was thick with humidity, the sunlight buttery and golden as it flooded the workshop. The silence stretched on as the mirror melded with the stone from the land of Tenebris, recognizing it as now part of itself.

By that evening the mirror was nearly complete. The frame was fully constructed, the refractive surface hummed, and the stone sat in its anchoring place. It was extraordinary. Seraphine knew that it would be, by the way the work felt. Soft, threadlike patterns scattered over the walls of the workshop that moved when she moved and stilled when she stilled.

The mirror had gone somewhere she had not entirely

designed. It was patient, warm, and extraordinary, and she understood that the work had been in conversation with her for the past two days, but she had been too occupied with other things to hear what it was saying.

She heard it now, but she did not yet understand what it meant.

Seraphine covered the mirror carefully with a drop cloth. She went downstairs to her apartment, washed up, ate, and got ready for bed. She would complete the mirror in the morning.

She did not know, lying in the dark, that she would not finish it tomorrow.

# CHAPTER
# TWENTY-ONE

Seraphine stood at her bench, ready to begin the last phase of work on the mirror, when she heard footsteps on the stairs she recognized. Valdris. He moved through spaces with easy authority of someone who had decided in advance that his presence was expected and welcome. Someone who would not accept no for an answer. More footsteps followed. He'd brought others with him.

She glanced at the mirror, which she had uncovered. It shone and hummed in the morning light, sending threads of light dancing throughout the space.

A knock sent the light scattering. Seraphine did not have time to note how it dissipated, responding to the intrusion. She set down her tools and answered the door.

He came through with the two junior council staff behind him, both carrying portfolios, and Mira, who bore a pinched expression of apology. Valdris handed her a folded document before he had fully crossed the workshop.

"The council's oversight protocol for the commission," he said. "Effective immediately."

Seraphine unfolded it and read it at her bench while he waited. The directive cited three subsections of the commission framework governing large-scale civic artificer projects and required written progress reports, as well as periodic inspections of the work by a council-approved delegation. The language was formal. It had been written by someone who understood the laws regarding government projects well enough to make the requirement look standard. It seemed that Valdris had taken personal offense to her uncovering his use of bureaucratic filing and had thrown it back in her face.

"This clause is not in the original commission terms," she said.

Valdris spread his arms in a gesture that he presumed was welcoming and friendly. He didn't have his wings, so he defaulted to using his arms to convey his intentions. "The council has the authority to implement oversight protocols on civic commissions of this scale at any stage of the work. The framework provision is cited on the second page."

Mira shifted slightly on her feet, the only sign of her discomfort. The two junior councilors were unfazed.

Seraphine turned to the page and quickly found the provision. She had not encountered it before because she had not worked on a commission of sufficient scale, or political sensitivity, to trigger it.

It was not standard, that much was certain. She had worked on six major civic commissions her career and none of them had included a. Mid-construction inspection. Those clauses existed in the framework for projects where the commissioning body had reason to suspect the work was deviating from their original specifications. Valdris and the council had no such cause.

What he had was a mirror that was three-quarters complete, and a woman working alone who had a copy of a suppressed report sewn into the lining of her coat pocket and had told him she'd decided what to do with it when the mirror was complete.

She folded the directive and set it on the bench. "The first inspection. When would you like it to take place?"

"Today, if you are willing. We're here," he said in a tone that left no room for argument. He had framed his ambush as a courtesy and was waiting to see if she would accept the pantomime.

Seraphine decided to play along. She stepped aside and gestured to the nearly complete mirror.

Mira opened the notebook she carried and held her pen above the paper, ready to document. The two junior councilors merely watched, witnesses to this now formal council visit.

"The work is on schedule," Seraphine said.

Valdris stepped closer to the frame. "Yes. The council would like to understand the current stage of construction, if you'd be so kind. For our records."

She showed him the frame and explained the load-bearing and thermal regulation components, choosing her words carefully. She gave him the technically accurate description but did not reveal the mechanism. She showed him the mirror glass and noted its distribution without specifically mentioning Ossin's length of woven light. She described the current stage of completion in precise percentages without telling him what the mirror would do when it was finished.

Mira took her notes diligently. Seraphine noted the way her pen skittered across the page and made sure to use sentences that would look thorough on a report but would be useless to anyone trying to replicate her work.

Valdris was good enough to know she was doing it, but not good enough to know how to stop her because the information she was withholding was technical, specific to her craft, and he was not an artificer.

"This here in the base structure," he said, eyeing the pre-separation stone that hovered in the gap that needed to be filled. "That is not a standard material, correct?"

"It's a specialist material sourced through the guild's historical holdings registry." This was only adjacently accurate, but Seraphine had no qualms about this level of deception. "The anchoring function requires a specific resonance that standard materials don't carry."

"And the council would have access to documentation on this material?"

"The material will be documented under my progress report under anchoring structure components." She would note that the material existed, but nothing else. "If the council has a specific technical question about the material or structure, I am happy to answer in writing. For your report."

Valdris paused for a heartbeat. "That would be helpful," he said.

Seraphine nodded and looked at him from across her bench. The mirror's surface projected threadlike movement on the walls, taking in the bright summer light and enhancing it. She watched him decided the pressing further would produce nothing useful.

He offered her a saccharine smile. "The council appreciates your cooperation."

"Of course."

Valdris gathered his staff, closing their meeting. The portfolios were closed. Mira capped her pen. She was the last to leave, following the junior staff through the door. As she passed the bench, she gave Seraphine a small smile. Then she was gone, and Seraphine heard four sets of footsteps descending the stairs and the street door closing.

She stood in the empty workshop, watching the light dance across the walls. Then she picked up her tools and got back to work.

HER HANDS MOVED through the sequence of enchantment she had designed and refined over the weeks of her failed models. Her mind was still as her attention focused solely on placing the preservation enchantment on the mirror.

She thought of Eiran without meaning to. A mental image of him sitting across from her with his notebook open, looking at her expectantly, as if he'd just asked her an important question. The thought was involuntary, arriving without permission.

The mirror's surface moved.

Seraphine froze. The glass moved again, as if someone were grazing a hand from the inside of a curtain. It was there and gone in the space of a breath. Seraphine stood very still, hands poised above the mirror, mind still focused on the precise spot in her enchantment sequence.

She looked at the movement the way she studied unexpected behavior in materials: for cause, for what it indicated about the structure, for whether it was a problem or a property. She had been thinking about Eiran. The mirror had moved. The correlation was clear. Seraphine set it aside, the way she set aside variables she could not yet account for and continued.

~

HER SECOND WARNING came as the afternoon light began to shift towards evening. Seraphine was nearing the very last sequence of enchantment. She felt the frequency reverberating through her entire body. The glass sung disc did its work, calibrating the frequency of the mirror's magical output to something she had never experienced. It was not frightening, simply new. Her hands moved on their own. The work was going well.

Eiran arrived again, completely and all at once. His face, his hands, the tenor of his voice as he read aloud to her. The bright hazel of his eyes, matching the hues of his frayed coat. She pictured him so clearly, as if he was standing next to her.

The mirror blazed and she stepped back from it, hands up. Something internal that was neither light nor heat radiated outward from the glass. There was a depth to the surface that had not been there, a consciousness directed outwards. It lasted for three seconds. Then it was gone, and the mirror was simply the mirror. Extraordinary and still, the thread-patterns of light still on the walls.

Seraphine noted in her working log: *Second anomalous response. Duration: three seconds. No structural compromise detected. Monitor.* Then she set down her pen and continued where she had left off.

She completed the final sequence, sealing her hours of work behind a protective enchantment that would prolong the life of the materials, guarding against the elements and the inevitably jostling that would come with the journey ahead.

Twenty minutes later, the mirror was finished. It was the most extraordinary thing she had ever made. The mirror was alive, in the way art carried the breath of its creator, exceeding the intention that had produced it.

Seraphine set down her tools and wiped the sweat from her brow. She looked at the chair by the window. "I think it's going to work," she whispered.

The darkness did not answer her.

CHAPTER

# TWENTY-TWO

The delegation arrived the day after Seraphine submitted her written report. The mirror was finished, and the council wanted to inspect her work.

Aldaveth entered the workshop first, followed by the two junior staff with their portfolios clutched like talismans to their chests. A council archivist who was there to document the proceedings, two members of the city guard in pale cream municipal uniforms, followed. Valdris entered last, which was different from his usual habit of entering rooms before the fae he had brought with him. Seraphine noted the change without remarking on it.

The group stood and looked at the mirror. She had uncovered it that morning, the first time since she'd finished it two days ago. Seraphine had needed those two days for herself. She had written for report for the council, but had needed time to process, to simply exist in the presence of the most significant thing she had ever made. If felt like standing near something very vast, yet quiet. Like a standing at the edge of a reservoir in the dark, knowing the water was there, and deep, by its silence rather than by seeing it.

The delegation was quiet for much long than she had expected.

Aldaveth recovered first. He said the appropriate things. That the council appreciated her work, noting the significance of the achievement, and a formal acknowledgement for the archivist's sake that the commission was completed on schedule.

Seraphine listened without interruption.

Valdris said nothing for a long time. He stood slightly apart from the others, with something like genuine awe plastered on his face. Not the calculated warmth or guilt she had come to expect from him. She found she resented it more than any of his other qualities, because awe was the only thing he had shown her that she entirely believed.

"It is remarkable," he finally said.

"It does what it was built to do," Seraphine said.

Valdris turned to her. The awe receded, the calculation returned. "We'll depart in two days. The installation site in the third corruption zone has been identified by the survey team. I will accompany you personally, along with a guard detachment." He said this with the air of someone announcing a schedule rather than making a decision, which meant that this had been decided some time ago without her input. "The mirror will need to be secured for transport. The road to the southern pass is manageable by wagon for the first three days."

"I will build a transport crate today," Seraphine said. There was no point in arguing. The plans had clearly been set, and she knew they would see the mirror installed with or without her help. And she would be damned if they pushed her aside for an artificer of lesser talent to install the greatest thing she'd ever made. "I'll need it loaded under my supervision."

"Of course."

The junior staff and the archivist spoke in low voices, consulting their notes and portfolios. The council's record of the commission's completion was assembled in the careful institutional language of people for whom the record was the thing of most importance. The mirror was merely secondary.

When the delegation left, she stood in the workshop and looked at the mirror for a while longer. Then, she gently placed the drop cloth over it and set about building the transport crate.

Seraphine decided on straight-grained ash for stability, reinforced at the joints with resonance alloy and a strapping she cut and fitted herself. She lined with crate with undyed wool felt and the same cloth Thessaly Morn has used to wrap her glass disc. Some part of her had known she would need it for something.

Seraphine tested the crate's stability by loading it with weighted sandbags equivalent to the mirror's mass and pushing it across the workshop's floor. It was sound. She lifted the crate at one end, then another, testing how the weight distributed itself. It would do.

She uncovered the mirror. "You're going to be moved," she told it. "This will be temporary. The transport is well-built."

The afternoon sun hit the mirror's surface, and the threads of light scattered around the workshop. She had the impression that the mirror was listening to her, and understood every word, thought, and intention. This was no longer unsettling. It was simply one of the mirror's properties, like its warmth, weight, vibration, and the way the light inside it that had no optical explanation.

SERAPHINE PACKED THE MIRROR HERSELF, with Aldaveth's two junior staff present. They watched and did nothing else because she had told them clearly that their function was to observe, and that their observation did not include assistance. She wrapped the mirror in wool felt, then set it atop of Thessaly's cloth, which was spread out on the bottom of the crate, on top of the first layer of cushion.

The mirror was as tall as she was. She used a simple enchantment to lift the mirror from its place set against her workbench and lowered it into the crate. She packed more wool around it with deliberate care. After this, the mirror would no longer be hers. It would be anchored into the landscape, serving the purpose for which it was built.

She sealed the crate, marked it with her own notation rather than the council's which the junior staff noted in the record without comment.

They returned a few hours later with a party of the civic guard, who loaded the crate onto a wagon that waited in the street. Seraphine walked all the way downstairs with them and watched as they loaded the crate into the wagon, following her instructions. They treated the crate with care, which was the only thing that let her return the workshop, reassured that the council had given adequate instructions to safeguard their commission.

She closed the workshop the following morning, before the party assembled at the civic stables.

Seraphine closed the windows. All of them. For the first time she could remember, she stood at each one, pulled it shut, and latched it. They each clicked with a different sound, resonating in the silence of the workshop. The forge was cold. She'd swept out all the ashes. She covered the bench with canvas cloth and tied it at the corners. She looked at the shelves with their labeled jars in Eiran's handwriting and left them exactly as they were.

She stood at the top of the stairs with her hand on the door and had the strange feeling that she was not going to be coming back in a few weeks. The commission terms said nothing about an extended absence. She had no information that she was not returning. But she knew anyway, in the way she had felt in her bones that she cared deeply for a scholar in a fraying green coat who sat in her chair by the window.

She left a note for the bookbinder below, explaining that she would be traveling on council business, and that she expected to return in a matter of weeks. She sealed the note and slipped it under his door.

Seraphine picked up her pack and went downstairs. She did not look back at the workshop.

She walked next to the canal in the early hours of the morning, the sound of moving water and birdsong echoing through the trees that lined the bright, clean path.

The party was waiting for her at the civic stables. The mirror's crate was already loaded onto a wagon, solid and wide-wheeled, built for difficult terrain and pulled by two horses. Their coats were caramel-colored, and each head a blonde mane that had been nearly brushed which seemed wholly unnecessary, but Seraphine found it endearing. These horses were Durrochs. Not bred for riding, but for pulling heavy loads and navigating the difficult terrain of the mountain passes. They were large and muscled through the shoulder and hindquarters. They stood calmly at the front of the wagon, as they had done this sort of thing before and knew it was not worth being anxious about.

Seraphine walked to the horse nearest her and put her hand on its neck. It turned, fixing its large, warm-brown eye on her. She felt steadied.

One of the junior council staff, a young fae who had clearly never been south before, looked at the wagon and then at the assembled party. "Would it not be faster to—"

"No," said the guard captain, a blonde fae with pointed ears and golden eyes. She addressed the question with the patience of someone who had answered this before. "The corruption zones generate significant atmospheric pressure at the boundary regions. Wing function degrades in proportion to proximity. By the time you reach the second zone you would be grounded and expended the reserves you need for other things." She settled her pack. "We walk, and we ride. We do not fly."

The junior staff member noted something in his portfolio and said nothing further.

Seraphine had read the expedition accounts carefully, and every one of them noted the same thing. The corruption's interference with magical function began well before the visible mist, which meant the wing degradation started further north than most fae assumed. Eiran had noted it too, in his second letter. *The wings are useless past the first survey marker. I folded mine away two days before I anticipated I would need to.*

Valdris mounted his own horse, a black mountain horse with a shining coat and silver bridle. Six others, the guard, assembled. They wore their customary cream with swords at their belts, but they wore a collection of light cauldrons, leather jerkins, quilted vests, and bracers. Their typically ceremonial garb transformed into clothing that would actually protect them from harm, should they encounter any.

Aldaveth, who was not accompanying them, but who had still arrived to see them off, stood at the stable entrance. He offered a formal farewell that Seraphine received with a nod.

As they pulled out of the stable yard, Seraphine placed her hand against the crate, her palm fat against the ash planking. She felt the mirror's warmth through the wood.

They walked, heading south for the Durnath Pass, and for the corruption beyond it.

THE FIRST NIGHT, Seraphine slept in a roadside inn six hours south of Caeledrath, in a narrow room with a window that faced east. She lay in the dark and listened to the horses in the stable below and the sounds of other people settling into their nighttime routines. The building creaked, but not in the ways she was used to.

She dreamed of Eiran's green coat.

She was walking behind it; on a road she did not recognize. It moved away from her at a pace she could keep up with if she wanted to. At some point she wondered if it was Eiran wearing his coat, moving ahead of her.

Seraphine walked behind it for a long time. She did not call out to him, because she couldn't be sure if it was truly him. The distinction felt important.

She woke before the dawn and lay in the pale gray of early morning. Then she got up, dressed, and went to check on the crate on the wagon. The air was cold and she shivered as she walked to the stables. Gooseflesh covered her arms. She checked the joints, the binding, and was that everything was as it should be.

Seraphine put her hand on the crate, letting the warmth seep into her palm. She looked out, and the road south beckoning from beyond the inn yard.

Light, pale and thin, tinted the edges of the sky. She breathed, welcoming the dawn, and found she was ready to continue.

# TWENTY-THREE

The party reached the mouth of the pass on the fourth day, early in the afternoon.

The Durnath's rock wall rose on either side of side in horizontal bands of color that the sunlight caught at different angles. Deep ochre at the base, rust, then gray so dark it absorbed the light rather than returned it. Near the top, a pale stratum that was spotted with reflective chips of mica sparkled, inconsistent with the rock around it, as though something in its mineral content was different than everything below it. Seraphine counted seven distinct geological periods visible in the exposed rock face before the walls curved inward and blocked the view.

*The pass itself was extraordinary in its geological complexity.*

She had read that sentence repeatedly in Eiran's first letter. Standing at the mouth of the Durnath Pass with the horses patient behind her and the guard assembled in its crossing formation, she noted that what he had written was true.

Seraphine looked at the strata as Valdris readied himself,

mounting his own horse. She studied them as she would study materials, observing what they were and what they had been, their history compressed into their composition. These were old mountains. They had been dividing two worlds for longer than either world had recollection of, and they carried that history in their stone.

She put her hand on the rock at the pass entrance. Cold and dry, and underneath that a resonance she recognized. It felt the same as the stone used in the mirror's frame. There was something there, from before the severing when this mountain had been part of a continuous landscape, rather than serving as a boundary between two separated ones.

Seraphine took her hand away and shivered. She wrapped her cloak around her shoulders, returned to the wagon, and checked the crate strappings.

"We should move," Valdris said behind her.

"We should." She clicked her tongue at the Durrochs, who leaned into their harnesses without fuss.

The pass wall rose high, and the light overhead narrowed to a moving strip that shifted as the walls closed in, the stone changing character as the party descended. The pale luminous stratum passed above and gave way to the darker formations of the mountain's deeper layers. Rock that had never been near the surface, had never touched sunlight. The Durroch's hooves on the pass floor echoed, doubling in rhythm.

Midway through the first afternoon, the air changed. The shift was physical. There was a new weight to each breath, a complexity in what Seraphine drew into her lungs, as though Grauradur's air were composed of something lighter. Every kilometer of ground between the mountains and what lay further south lay in the air in this portion of the pass, insistent about being noticed.

She breathed it delicately, cataloguing it as she went, and said nothing of it to anyone.

They made camp, sheltering in a depressed area of the pass, like a giant hand had scooped out a portion of the wall, making room for tents, the wagon, and the horses. The fire took some encouragement, as though it did not want to be lit. When it did finally flare to life, it burned weakly. Seraphine noted this, too, and kept it to herself as she lay down on her bedroll, timing her breath with the horses.

The next day, they passed through the Durnath's southern mouth and into Tenebris. They were now in the first zone of corruption.

It was technically he same sun and sky. The light that reached the ground here had been reduced in its travel, diminished in the way of a lamp turned down rather than a lamp moved further away. The vegetation; shrub brush, fireweed, and bitterroot, ran deep green, shading towards black. The ground was dark, as though the landscape had forgone brightness entirely, letting its colors grow muted.

They walked, and Seraphine found the first signed of discoloration. The ground did not have the rich, compressed color of a healthy landscape, but a lifeless gray. As it something had been using itself up for a long time without being replenished. The air above the section of leeched ground hit the back of her mouth, tasting metallic.

Behind her, one of the guards cleared his throat. Another spat carefully over the side of the wagon track. Valdris had stopped talking.

The Durrochs walked through it without breaking their stride.

A few hours later, they reached zone two, and the mist. It arrived the way damp weather arrived, gradually then undeniably. The visibility dwindled as the wisps of fog at ground level accumulated as they moved deeper into the land, until the mist was thick and cloying.

The mist drifted slowly. It was unresponsive to the wind, or to the party moving through it. It moved according to its own logic.

Seraphine thought of Eiran's second letter. *More like watching weather than anything malicious.*

She agreed with him. Standing in it, breathing carefully through her nose, she found that her agreement was both a comfort and full of grief. She was verifying his field notes, taking the same journey he had taken, and he was not here for her to tell him that he had been right.

The corruption was not malicious, but it was spreading and making the air taste of old copper. It reduced the visibility and did things to ambient magic that she could feel as wrongness in the frequencies she was accustomed to reading, but it did not do so with evil intent. It behaved like a bad storm cloud, terrible, and consuming, but simple like weather.

The guard captain called a halt. Scarves were distributed from the supply pack, thick wool dampened from water flasks. The guards tied them over their faces with the practiced motion of a briefed unit. Valdris accepted his with an air of strained dignity.

Seraphine felt the familiar absence of her wings. She had not tried to summon them, but the part of her magical reserves that would have sustained them had gone dull and unresponsive, the way a limb grew numb in extreme cold. The corruption was affecting this basic ability of most fae.

Whatever the wings would have offered, they would not be offering it here.

Seraphine took her scarf and held it, breathing the mist directly and cataloguing what she found. The air was metallic, but also faintly acidic. Sustained exposure would begin to affect the lungs, according to expedition texts. It would be a slow, corrosive accumulation rather than an immediate effect. She tied the cloth over her nose and mouth.

The density of the fog increased in stages. Visibility went from twenty meters to ten, then from ten to the length of Seraphine's outstretched arm. The mist did not drift. It pressed inwards, smothering.

Then the Durroch nearest her screamed and jolted, rearing on its hind legs. A full, sustained scream, the sound of a creature that had encountered something its body recognized as fundamentally wrong and was responding with everything it had. The second horse answered immediately, and the wagon lurched as both animals tried to back away from the mist simultaneously, their hooves scrambling on the uneven ground, the whole rig pitching sideways as the harnesses pulled taut and held.

The captain shouted. Two of the guards lunged for the horses' heads, grabbing bridles, adding their weight against the animals' momentum. It was not enough. The Durrochs were large, and they were terrified. The wagon lurched again. Inside the crate, something shifted.

Seraphine pushed past the guard at the wagon's side and got her hands on the crate's latch. She had built the latching mechanism herself, and she could open it blindfolded, which was approximately the condition she was operating in. The latch released. She lifted the lid.

The horses bellowed and tried to rear, held down by both guards now.

She pulled back the outer layer of wool felt, then the cloth. She did not uncover the mirror fully. She did not need to, and she was not going to expose it to the corruption's density any further than necessary. She folded back enough to expose the upper portion of the frame and stepped back as the wagon jerked again.

The air immediately around the wagon that changed. The mist thinned within a radius of four meters. It didn't retreat, but it became less dense, slightly less pressing. The metallic taste at the back of Seraphine's throat reduced by a fraction.

Both horses were still trembling, their breath coming in hard audible pulls, the whites of their eyes visible in the murk. But they had stopped screaming and moving with blind fear. The horse nearest Seraphine turned its head toward the open crate with the instinctive orientation of an animal moving toward warmth, and stood, calmer.

The guard captain appeared at Seraphine's shoulder. He looked at the open crate, at the horses, at the thinned mist around them.

"Keep them close to the wagon," Seraphine said, before he could ask anything. "Stay close and don't let anyone fall behind it."

She looked at the exposed portion of the mirror's frame. The scrollwork caught what little light the mist permitted and held it, the light-weaving threaded through the metal did its work, even from within the crate. It was not designed for this, to work as an ambient counter to corruption, but it was doing it anyway.

Seraphine put her hand on the exposed frame briefly.

Then she pulled the cloth back over it, leaving a gap at the top where the frame's light could still reach the air around the wagon.

"We can move on," she said to the guard captain. "But slowly"

The Durrochs were coaxed into motion. They still trembled, their ears flat, their heads low. But they walked, soothed by the mirror's frame.

She kept one hand on the crate's edge for the remainder of the crossing.

Behind her, the guard walked in close formation, inside the radius, their scarves pulled over their faces. A young guard, whose name was Posy and who had watched her during the workshop inspection, turned her pale, sharp-featured face to the crate. Then to Seraphine. She said nothing, but Seraphine had noticed the spark of relief in her eyes.

Nobody spoke. The only sounds were the horses' breathing and the muffled percussion of hooves on ground they couldn't see.

THEY EMERGED from the third zone's densest region suddenly. Seraphine blinked, and the fog had thinned. The mist curled against an invisible wall, then stopped.

On the other side, the air was sharp with cold and pine resin. Seraphine pulled the scarf from her face and breathed deeply.

The landscape was rocky and steep, the mountain stone broke through the surface in long ridges that ran parallel to the Durnath's southern face. Coniferous forest covered the upper slopes, the old-growth pines centuries old and clustered together. A waterfall in the north roared ceaselessly, its dull thunder echoing across the land. As they crested the next rise she saw it, white against the dark rock face, dipping forty meters into a steel-blue pool. This land was wild and untamed, persistent even in the face of the corruption. Seraphine stared at it and understood why Eiran had loved it.

It was nothing like Grauradur, with its polish and carefully sculpted architecture. It was not ordered or luminous or concerned with elegance. Tenebris was rugged, complicated, and beautiful. It had worked very hard to stay alive for a long time and had developed its own fierceness in the process. Better than elegance, because it was earned.

Eiran had crossed the Durnath Pass because something in him knew this was worth crossing for. He had been right, and she was standing in it months too late, without him.

The horses lifted their heads for the first time in an hour and blew out long breaths, as though sighing with relief.

Seraphine stepped over to the wagon, pulled the cloth over the mirror, and replaced the wool. She latched the crate and checked the straps. It had been instinctual to uncover it. She had felt its warmth through the ash planks and known that its passive resonance would help. She had not designed it to function that way, but it had done so regardless.

She readjusted her pack, and walked forward, letting the mist from the waterfall tickle her face and the pine in the air clear her lungs.

Seraphine found the installation site the following morning. She walked the terrain for three hours before she found the spot, letting it find her more than she actively searched for it, the same was she approached difficult problems. The landscape here required her to think about the puzzle in a new way. Her Caeledrath instincts for material and light were accurate here, but needed recalibrating, the way a precision instrument needed recalibrating when the ambient conditions changed.

She stopped when she reached a natural shelf of exploded mountain stone, south-facing and elevated enough to have a clear view of the surrounding landscape in three directions. The stone on this shelf was a different color from the surrounding outcrops, paler and humming with magic. When she crouched and placed her palm to the stone it hummed with the same quality as Ossin's cedar box, Meras's stone fragment, and Thessaly's glass sung-disc. Seraphine got the distinct impression that the ground was prepared and waiting for her arrival. Over the last decades of artificer work, Seraphine had learned to take the feeling seriously when it arose.

She marked the site with a cairn she built from spare rocks and went back to camp.

The guards carried the crate to the shelf with renewed care. They had seen the way the crate had repelled the corruption when they were in its densest parts and now understood what lay inside it. Seraphine opened the crate herself and using her weightless enchantment, set it on the exposed stone and stepped back.

She had built the mirror in a Caeledrath workshop in the light that came off the canal, with Eiran's notebook on her bench beside her tools. Seeing it here, in the landscape it had been made for, was different from all of that. The light on the stone caught the mirror's surface, and the surface immediately began to interact with it. The refractive structure engaged with the available light and sent it outward in threads too fine to see individually, perceptible only as a sensation in the air around them, a presence that had not been there before.

Seraphine put her hands on the frame. The final step in the mirror's creation was the binding to the landscape. This was the opening of the mirror outward, the anchoring on of to the specific landscape it had been made for, the point at which the mirror would stop being a made thing and become something the land would incorporate, the way soil incorporated root systems, taking the forming structure in and making it a part of itself.

She identified the first anchoring point in the stone beneath her feet, the place where the shelf's pale rock met the resonance of the pre-separation fragment in the mirror's base. The frequency recognized itself in the ground it was being given to. She put her hands flat on the frame and began.

CHAPTER
# TWENTY-FOUR

Seraphine felt the deepening connection between her hands, the mirror's frame, and the rugged landscape around her. The awareness of Valdris and the guard she'd felt when she first began the binding gradually faded until there was nothing but her, the mirror, and her work. The stone beneath her feet added its resonance to the exchange, and the stone in the mirror's base responded to the ground of the rock shelf, the frequencies matching just as she'd intended. There was no technical term for it, other than *rightness*. The physical sensation of a material finding what it had always been compatible with and settling into it.

The anchoring deepened with each pass of her enchantment. Her palms grew warm, echoing the warmth in the mirror's frame.

Below the shelf, at the edge of the mirror's passive clearing radius, the corruption's discoloration was visible in the landscape. The grey spent color of the affected ground, the reduced light above it. The boundary between the cleared and corrupted air was visible as a slight shift in the

184

atmosphere, like the boundary of two bodies of water with different temperatures.

The mirror's surface changed as she worked.

The pulling came from inside the mirror rather than the ground. Seraphine felt the distinction clearly; the same way she felt the distinction between a material's surface and its structure when she was reading a piece. The ground was pulling the mirror's light outward, as designed. But something inside the mirror was pulling toward her, and the directions were different.

Her hands were still against the frame. The mirror waited.

She had read about the offering principle twice, in two separate texts, and she had understood the distinction between the vessel and the soul. The vessel was complete. The woven light, the sung disc, and the stone had built something that could hold magic and distribute it. But the mirror had been showing her, for months, what it still needed. In the workshop, every time she had spoken to the empty chair and the mirror's surface had shifted in response. Every time she had thought of Eiran and felt the mirror reach back. She had looked away from what that meant because she had not been ready for it.

She was ready now.

The mirror was waiting. It had always been waiting, with the patience of something that understood it could not become what it was meant to be without her. The offering principle had told her this in plain language: it cannot be taken. It must be given, and the giving must be chosen, or the work remains only itself and does not become more than itself.

Seraphine diagnosed what the mirror needed the way she diagnosed everything, by testing for function.

Not her memories of Eiran. She checked, and every recollection of him was present and accounted for. The green coat, the milk jug, the handwriting on the jars slanting left. The last morning. All of it intact and undisturbed.

Nor was it taking her knowledge of her love for him. She tested this, too, pressing at it as she would a joint, she suspected of weakness, and it held. She had loved Eiran Vael. She loved him. That remained.

What the mirror needed was the function that connected those memories to the living world.

She understood it clearly now. When she encountered something in the world that carried his quality the memories and the love would reach outward through that function and find him there, present and irreplaceable. The function was the bridge. The part that kept him alive in the world rather than only in her head. The part of love that refused to stay inside the person who felt it and kept going outward, finding the beloved in things.

The mirror needed her living, emotional connection to Eiran, and it was asking her to give it.

Seraphine knew she stood at a crossroads. With her hands on the frame and considered her options. She thought about the specific cruelty of finding Eiran in the small, mundane areas of her life. When she made two cups of tea instead of one or saw someone reading with an intense expression that reminded her of him and feeling the full weight of his absence in the same breath. The grief that caught her at the canal in the mornings, in the light on the water. The way she had never stopped looking for him in a world that no longer contained him.

She thought about where that connection to him would go, if she gave it. Into the mountain stone beneath her feet, and the pine-scented air of this rugged and complicated landscape. Into the light that moved across the ridgelines as though it was interested in what it illuminated. His way of being, distributed into the world he had loved. Translated into something that would outlast both of them by centuries.

This was not resignation or the surrender of someone who had run out of choices. It was the decision of a person who had spent fifteen years learning the difference between what work required and what it deserved, and who understood that the greatest things she had ever made had always cost the most specific and irreplaceable parts of herself. The Aldenmere lenses. The Thaumic Meridian she had built for a scholar in a fraying green coat who had asked her questions she couldn't stop thinking about.

The mirror waited.

Seraphine pressed her hands flat against the frame and let it enter the mirror. She felt the living, breathing connection to him leave her in threads, fine as the ones the mirror was sending into the ground, and she let each one go. This was not different from any other making. It was the completion of it.

Her hands began to move again through the final sequence of the enchantment, the last passes, and she talked to him while she worked.

As her hands slowed in their movements, the magic ebbing from her, she thought about Eiran. He would have found the cost worth paying. The way he listened, his compassionate attention, the way he had made every person he spoke to feel like the most interesting person in any room, distributed into the land he had crossed a mountain range to understand. In the light that moved through the rugged and pine-scented landscape. In the ground beneath her feet, which was already receiving all of it, incorporating it into whatever the land was in the process of becoming. He would have found that worth paying.

"I love you," she whispered, because here, in this moment, the truth was important.

The anchoring deepened, the mirror's refractive structure extending itself into the mountain in threads she felt but didn't see, fine and persistent. The living light began to distribute itself into ground that had been waiting for it for centuries.

"I left without telling you that on the last morning, and I have been carrying it since. I am setting it down now. Not because it no longer matters. Because it matters enough to give."

The pine forest above the shelf was motionless. No wind blew. The guard and Valdris behind her stood frozen still. It almost felt like time had slowed, the mirror giving her this last opportunity to say goodbye.

She continued talking in a low voice as she completed the last rites of anchoring. "You reorganized my supply jars, and my kitchen shelf. I never moved anything back and I'm not going to."

The mirror hummed louder, though she was certain she was the only one who could hear it.

"You were the best argument I ever lost, because you were right. This mirror is proof that there is a difference between discipline and feeling, and you're not here to be insufferable about that. It is one of the more specific injustices of the situation."

The mirror glass rippled in the same way it had in her workshop. Exhaustion pulled at Seraphine's limbs, her eyelids. She was nearly done.

"This mirror is made of light and love and three things that were given freely by fae who understood that some objects are not constructed but given into being. It's made of you."

Seraphine made the final passes over the mirror frame. The mirror and the land slid into place, locking together forever.

"The Aetheris Mirror. Aetheris means living light, which seems fitting. You believe in living light even when you were walking into the dark to study it. This is how you will be remembered, Eiran. You will be not just mine anymore, but a part of all things."

The mirror and the land locked into place.

She felt the last connection to him leave her as the last binding sealed into place. The wind stirred in the trees, carrying the bite of resin through the air once more. A single tear dripped down her cheek. It was not like losing a memory, leaving a gaping hole where he had been. More like a recalibration of her innermost self, the one that found Eiran everywhere she looked. That part of her grew quiet. That reaching for him, recognizing his qualities in strangers or finding him in the way the light reflected off the canal, had been woven into the threads the mirror was sending into the mountain stone, the crisp air, and the landscape that had been waiting for it.

Seraphine stood with her hands on the frame, feeling the new stillness inside herself. It was the silence of a completed thing, the specific peace that came at the end of work she had put all her effort into. She had made the most significant thing she would ever make, and she had given it everything it required, and it was done. The mirror and the mountain stone hummed at the same frequency, resonating with the light she had given it. It needed nothing more from her. A single tear tracked down her cheek. She did not wipe it away.

She lifted her hands from the frame and stepped back.

Behind her the guard and Valdris waited in trained stillness. The Durroch horses breathed steadily in the cold air. The corruption's discoloration held its position at the edge of the clearing radius, grey and patient.

Then the clouds above the shelf broke. A seam opened in the overcast, thirty meters wide, and through it came direct sunlight, the kind that had not reached this part of Tenebris in longer than anyone present could have calculated. It hit the mirror's surface, and the mirror refracted it outward in every direction. Downward into the stone, across the corrupted boundary, upwards into the air. The threads of anchored light reached into a landscape that drank it up the way dry ground received the first rain.

The corruption began to recede slowly, like an ebbing tide. The sunlight held, the mirror shone, weaving golden threads into the landscape. Seraphine felt one brush her cheek, drying away the tear that had fallen. Her skin hummed where it had touched her. She felt lighter.

Seraphine stood on the mountainside with her hands at her sides, the light on her face, and felt the clean quiet inside herself. She looked at the Aetheris Mirror and thought that Eiran would have called it extraordinary.

# TWENTY-FIVE

Footsteps on the stone, deliberate and unhurried, echoed behind Seraphine. She didn't bother turning around. She stared at the corruption boundary, watching it recede centimeters at a time. The corruption would not clear overnight, but it would leave and resolve, reintegrating back into the land, no longer starved of the magic it needed.

Valdris stopped beside her. "It's working," he said.

"It is."

He looked out at the dense fog with her and stood silent. She wondered if he was genuinely moved, or simply calculating. She was inclined to think the later.

"The council is grateful," he said. "What you have done here is significant. Whatever else is true, I want you to understand that I know that this is because of your efforts."

Seraphine turned to look at the mirror. The seam in the low clouds let in the sunlight, which hit the mirror and refracted, just as she'd intended. It would hold onto the light, even when the sun set and take in the moon's glow in its stead. It did what she designed it to do.

"What do you want, Valdris?"

He did not perform surprise at her directness. "The mirror requires a steward. Someone with the technical knowledge to monitor its function over time, to catch any failures before they happen. The council's position is that you are the only person qualified to do this."

He met her gaze openly, as he had prepared his position carefully and it was unassailable. Seraphine read past the surface of it. The suppressed report was the true reason behind his positioning. She had told him that she would decide what to do with it once the mirror was installed. If she returned to Caeledrath, she would make her decision, and Valdris could not afford what she might do.

This council appointment, technically an honor, was framed as necessity rather than the exile that it was.

Seraphine's eyes slid from Valdris's carefully composed face to the land. The pine-covered slopes, the rocky ridge-lines, and the waterfalls audible in the north. The quality of the light, lower and more considered than the light in Caeledrath.

She thought about her workshop on the canal, the windows she had opened every morning for fifteen years, the sounds the building made, the creaking stairs that announced the arrival of patrons. The empty chair by the window, the book on the sill. The bookbinder below, who left strawberry preserves on her doorstep every Winter Solstice, who would find the workshop closed and the building continuing to exist because the guild would pay for it with no explanations.

Seraphine thought also of Mira Aster, who by now would

have the copied report that Seraphine had sent from the inn before they'd crossed into the Durnath. Mira would know what to do with it. Not today, not perhaps for years, but she would use it eventually in the way that people who understood institutions understood how to move within them toward something true.

Seraphine had done all she could. What came next in Caeledrath was no longer hers to manage.

She closed her eyes briefly, letting the resinous, crisp air flood her lungs as she inhaled. When she opened them and looked at Valdris, she did not argue. The anger that burned like a hot coal in her stomach was hers to keep. She did not want to give him the satisfaction of sharing that anger. She had given everything to this commission. And he had taken away the very last thing from her.

The mirror was here. Eiran was here, distributed into the mountain stone, the air, the forest. The land now carried him, and she was being told she must remain in it. Remaining in Tenebris was not entirely a punishment. She would not give Valdris the satisfaction of knowing that, either, but it was true.

"I'll need the contents of my workshop shipped from Caeledrath. The full inventory. Tools, materials, reference texts, everything. Transported under the guild's supervision, not the council's."

"Agreed."

"I need a formal stipend at an extended civic commission rate, signed by the council and the guild."

"Of course."

"And I need to send a letter before your party leaves."

He nodded. He had what he wanted, the details were no unimportant.

She left him standing on the rocky shelf and crossed to where the guard assembled near the tree line. The young woman, Posy, stood slightly apart from the others, which Seraphine had noticed her doing throughout the journey. She had been watching Seraphine closely since the Durnath, as though she had set out with assumptions about what an artificer was and was quietly revising them in light of available evidence.

Seraphine stopped in front of her. "I need a letter carried to Caeledrath and I need to guarantee it will be delivered. Not sent through the council's courier system."

Posy's eyes flicked briefly to Valdris. "I can do that," she said, in a voice that was light as spring. She did not ask who the letter was for or pose any other questions. She simply agreed, and Seraphine was grateful.

Seraphine took the notebook from her pack and wrote standing up. Two words, and two words only. *It works.* She folded the note and wrote Professor Meras's name and department on the front. She had promised him. She kept her promises.

She handed it to Posy. "Thank you."

The guard nodded once and tucked it carefully into her breast pocket.

Seraphine returned to her pack and put her notebooks inside. She picked it up, settled the straps, and looked at the Aetheris Mirror one more time.

It stood erect on the pale stone in the afternoon light. The air around it carried the faint tang of magic. Seraphine put her hand on the frame as she would a doorframe of a room she was leaving, acknowledging the space before she moved through it. Then, she walked away from the shelf and into the forest.

She did not say goodbye to Valdris, nor did she look back at him. He was a variable she had accounted for and set aside.

The land was rugged. The waterfalls grew louder as she moved north, descending the shelf in a series of switchbacks. The light on the mountain stone caught the pale ridgelines, making the bright against the darker slopes above. Her pack was not heavy. She had always traveled light and had always understood that what mattered fit in a pack, and what didn't was what you had to learn to leave.

The nearest settlement, Varneth, was a day's hike northward. She had read about it in the survey team's documentation. It was a working community of about two hundred fae. Small, in the foothills were the ground leveled briefly before the next ridge. She had food for two days, water, and tools in a roll and the worn letter in her inner pocket. The small oval of resonance alloy, the filter she'd made all those months ago, was in her coat pocket.

Seraphine walked through the landscape, and the land received her without ceremony or question.

She reached Varneth the next day, her feet sore and her pack lighter than it had been, having eaten through most of her two days of provisions on the walk.

The settlement had been carved into the mountain rather than built against it. The buildings were cut directly from the dark granite of the lower ridge face, their walls the stone of the mountain itself, shaped and smoothed and fitted with timber frames and deep-set windows that kept the worst of the weather out without surrendering the rock's natural insulation. Some of the older structures had no separate walls at all. The mountain was the wall, and the inhabitants had simply hollowed out what they needed and lived inside it. The rooflines were low and irregular, following the natural contours of the ridgeline.

There was also the moss. It grew in deliberate lines along the outer walls of houses and the cobbled streets, packed into carved channels that ran at eye level around every building's exterior. It glowed, though not with any sort of crafted enchantment. A soft, persistent blue-green light, the color of shallow water held against the sky. It pulsed very slowly, at a rate just below what the eye could comfortably track. Where the channels met at corners the glow intensified slightly, as though the moss communicated with itself around the bends.

Seraphine stopped walking and looked at it.

A woman passing with a basket of something that smelled of dried mushrooms noticed her looking and paused. "Duskweed," she said, with a matter-of-fact tone. "It keeps the mist honest. It won't grow anywhere the corruption's gotten a proper hold, so if a channel goes dark, you know the boundary's moved."

She walked on before Seraphine could respond.

Seraphine looked at the moss channels running along the nearest building's exterior. An early warning system, grown rather than built, calibrated to the specific magical conditions of the landscape. She wondered how long it had taken them to work that out.

She continued up the lane toward the inn, whose chimney smoke was pine-scented and whose exterior channels of duskweed glowed a steady, uninterrupted blue-green.

The boundary had not moved here. That was something.

Everything else about Varneth was comfortably ordinary. A cobbled lane cut through the settlement's center. A mill set on the banks of a stream, turned by a cool and silver ribbon of cutting through the mountainside. The ambient sounds of people working, talking, going about their days floated through the air, echoing off the stone and carried by the crisp breeze.

Seraphine adjusted her pack and walked up the lane.

# TWENTY-SIX

Five years later, the workshop still surprised her sometimes, much in the way that a new material sometimes revealed unexpected properties after sustained work. Properties that weren't flaws but weren't what she'd planned for either.

Seraphine's workshop in Caeledrath had no surprises after the years she'd spent in it. She had known its every sound, every draft that came through the window, the way the light moved across her bench. This workshop she was still learning. This, she concluded, was not a deficiency, but simply the condition of being somewhere new.

The building was a converted storage room on the lane's eastern end, cut from the same dark granite as everything else in Varneth. Its walls were made of the mountain's own stone. The ceiling was lower than she would have chosen and followed the natural slope of the rock above, which meant the north end of the workshop was a full hand's width lower than the south end. Anything she stored on the north shelving needed to be measured for clearance. The floor was worn smooth by decades of previous use, cold underfoot in the mornings until the forge had been running long enough to push some warmth into the stone.

She had carved her own duskweed channel into the exterior wall in the second year, following the instruction of the innkeeper on depth and the direction of light exposure for the moss to establish. It had taken most of a season to take hold. Now it ran steadily along the workshop's outer face, visible from the lane. Over time, she had come to understand that this was its own kind of signal to the community: the artificer's workshop was open, the boundary was holding, everything was as it should be.

She had adapted.

The neighbor was a woman named Telma who had left a pot of stew on her doorstep after she'd moved in that was the best thing Seraphine had eaten in Varneth to that point, which she acknowledged by leaving the clean pot on Telma's doorstep the following morning. Since then, they'd had occasional exchanged of goods or food, but had never processed to conversation, which suited both.

Rina had appeared in the workshop doorway in the fourth year of Seraphine's residence with an expression of someone who had decided to do something and was not going to be dissuaded from it. She was the daughter of a surveyor who contracted Seraphine's work twice a year. Rina had not asked to be taught. She'd stood near the door and watched, asked nothing, and left when the working day ended. She had been doing this for weeks, and Seraphine had not told her to stop, which was its own kind of conversations.

One afternoon, Seraphine wordlessly held out a pair of wire cutters to her. Rina had been watching her make a compass for the past day. Seraphine had made a few in the time that Rina had observed her and knew what came next in the process. Rina took up the wire cutters, cut the length of copper correctly the first time and affixed it to the instrument, which is how Seraphine acquired an apprentice.

The innkeeper, a fae named Davan who had a slight permanent squint of someone who had done accounts in poor light, had stopped saying "What can I get for you?" When Seraphine came in and had started simply pouring what she usually had. In Varneth, this was the equivalent of an embrace.

These were not the relationships she'd had in Caeledrath. They were not close in any way she would have previously recognized, but they were real.

Seraphine washed her hands at the basin on a morning in early autumn, the Varneth air coming through the west window with pine-resin sharpness. She put the kettle on and took two cups from the shelf. She didn't notice until the tea was already steeping.

She stood at her bench and looked at the two cups for a long time. The steam rose from the full one. The empty one sat beside it, the same way the cups had sat on her bench in Caeledrath. This workshop was not that one. The light coming in was Tenebris's, the kind that had to work harder for what it illuminated.

Seraphine put the empty cup back on the shelf. Then she picked up her tea and went to the window.

Telma's door was open, which meant she was already in her garden. Rina crested the top of the lane, coming down with the deliberate pace of someone with a destination but who wasn't in a hurry. The mill on the stream thrummed its rhythm a bit faster, as the river was swollen with autumn rains. Above the mill, the pine-covered hillside caught the morning light, making the ridgeline's pale stone shine against the darker green above it.

Seraphine watched the light against the stone. At this hour, it was extraordinary. She had noticed this the first week she had moved in and had admired it ever since. The light moved across the ridgeline the way it moved across everything in Tenebris, with undivided attention, as though it was interested in what it was illuminated and had decided to take its time.

Seraphine turned back to the bench, set down her tea, and picked up her tools.

She was alright. She wasn't recovered, because that would imply she had returned to her prior state, and she had no interest in that. She wasn't healed either, because the wound was not closed. She wasn't sure if wounds of such size ever closed entirely, nor was she sure if they were supposed to. She had poured a significant portion of herself into the ground of a foreign land and remained to watch what grew. She was functional in a way that had become routine, and she was present in a place that was slowly becoming hers. She was alright.

The door swung open and Rina joined her, wordlessly watching to see what they would make today.

Seraphine handed her a jar of silver dust and watched her measure the material.

Outside, the light on the stone continued, patient, specific, and full of an attention she had stopped trying to name.

# TWENTY-SEVEN

Time progressed, and Seraphine found she had built something in Varneth she had not planned and would not have predicted.

It was different from her life in Caeledrath, which had been ordered, solitary, and sufficient. Here, the market on the mornings hummed with closeness and sold things that were new to her. Root vegetables that she had learned to cook with, and soft cheese made by a farm on the eastern ridge. There was Rina, who turned out to have a gift for resonance work that Seraphine was now in the process of learning to trust. Her quarterly walks to the mirror. Telma's continued gifts of food, which Seraphine returned by making her small things in return and occasionally sitting on the law wall overlooking her garden in the evening with a glass of mead.

And there was Reed.

She had not named this in the first year of noticing him because putting a name to it made it real in a way that required some sort of action, and she was not ready for that.

He ran the mill on the stream and had lived in Varneth his whole life. He'd chosen to stay, rather than failed to leave as the corruption grew closer to the settlement. He had wavy black hair that he kept tied in a knot, and strong forearms. He was patient and kind. He was present, without an agenda, and seemed in no hurry for Seraphine to see what was in front of her.

She was not ready, though she was closer to readiness than she ever thought possible. She understood that something might happen in its own time, and that it would never be what she and Eiran had been, but it did not need to be.

Her work had changed, too. The pieces she made in Varneth were heavier than the pieces she'd made in Caeledrath, as though each commission was being filtered through something unseen before it reached her hands. She did not yet fully understand what it was, other than perhaps the land itself. The years of quarterly walks through terrain that was no Grauradur's ordered elegance required her full attention. The fact that she had made the most significant thing she would ever make and everything that came after was still in conversation with that fact, whether she intended it or not.

Fae in Varneth said her work felt like it was breathing. She didn't tell them that she'd heard that before, she simply accepted it.

The quarterly reports to the guild documented the corruption's recession with a precision she always brought to documentation. Four kilometers since the installation, measured at six survey points along the boundary perimeter. The rate was consistent and showed no signs of plateauing. She noted it with satisfaction. The Aetheris was performing its function, which was worth something.

She had not heard from Valdris in six years. Seraphine did not expect that to change, which was fine with her.

SERAPHINE MADE her autumn walk to the mirror early in the morning. She paused at the top of the lane before beginning the descent to the path, as she always did, and looked at the duskweed channels running along the buildings below. When she had first arrived, the channels on the southernmost buildings had been running dim. The moss told anyone who knew how to read it that the boundary was close and the conditions were unfavorable. She had noted it in her first quarterly report.

Now, the southernmost buildings ran as steadily as the rest. The moss did not know about the Aetheris Mirror. It only knew about the light in the ground, and the light in the ground had changed, and the moss had responded to that change the way living things responded to improved conditions, which was by thriving.

She took out her notebook and recorded it. Then she walked on. The sun streamed through the early morning mist that curled at her feet and kissed the pines. It was a different mist that the one brewed by corruption. This was simply a product of weather and low-pressure systems and was quickly dissipating as the sun crested over the ridgeline. The deciduous trees flared amber and rust between the pines. It still surprised her, seven years in, how Tenebris in autumn shifted towards gold in the low light of the season, the stone ridgelines catching the sun different than they did in summer. The waterfalls sounded different, too, gradually growing softer as the summer rains dwindled and the peaks became snowcapped.

She had come to love the land. She knew which ridges gave the first view of the installation site, where the path grew soft after rain, and where the stone came through the surface and held firm regardless. She knew the pine at the two-hour mark of her hike that always smelled stronger than the surrounding forest. Something in the resin concentration from that specific grove was sharp and heady. The place where the path crossed a stream and the stepping-stones shone through as the water levels dropped.

Seraphine had walked this path in every season and knew it the way she knew things she had made, from the inside.

The mirror came into view suddenly after climbing that series of switchbacks and cresting the last ridge. The pale stone shelf was unchanged, supporting the mirror that caught the autumn light.

It was still extraordinary. The years had not diminished it. If anything, they had deepened the connection between the mirror and the mountainside, the anchoring sequence having taken root and merged the frame with the stone it sat on.

Seraphine set down her pack and looked at it. She had made it from grief and love, and three things given freely by fae who had understood the gravity of their gifts. The Aetheris was made from an irreplaceable weight of love that had nowhere left to go and had, in the end, gone into the ground of the land that had taken the person that love was for.

She could see that in the mirror. Not in a technical sense, but in a more subtle manner. She stood at the ridge for a while, then took out the binoculars she had crafted, adjusting their knobs and filters. She noted the distance of the corruption. the wall of pale gray fog further back than it had been at her last quarterly visit. The Aetheris Mirror did its patient work. It had a very long time to finish its job.

Seraphine took out her notebook and recorded the distance and documented her field notes, noting the season, the quality of the light, the levels of ambient magic in the air. She put aside her instruments and ran her checks on the mirror. It did not need them, but she was thorough. When she was finished, she returned her notebook to her pack.

Then, she put her hand on the frame briefly, as she always did, before she walked home.

# ACKNOWLEDGMENTS

If you are reading this book, then you have my immeasurable thanks. This novella is the product of many wonderful interactions with readers, romantasy lovers, and book clubs. Not a day goes by that I don't appreciate all you do for authors and the indie book community.

To my husband, Adam, whose unending belief in me and support has allowed me to pursue my dreams.

To Maddie, whose editorial skills saved me from any potential typo embarrassment. Em for making me my very first ever custom bound book (you rock). To David, Matt, and Phoebe - the kindest podcasters I've ever met. To librarians, booksellers, and book influencers who continue to spread the joy of reading. Your work is important and appreciated.

# ABOUT THE AUTHOR

Cidney Mayes is a fantasy author whose work weaves dark, atmospheric worlds with fierce heroines and forbidden knowledge. Based in Portland, Maine, she is a teacher librarian and MFA in Creative Writing candidate at Southern New Hampshire University. When not writing, you can find her wandering wooded paths, playing boardgames, or watching reality TV with her husband and cats. You can connect with her at cidneymayes.com.